Bolan unlimbered his Steyr AUG

He was ready to rock at the first sign of danger. He couldn't be sure if the target was where he'd been told it would be. Things changed, day-to-day, and his intelligence might have been faulty to start with. Still, it was the only lead he had, the only fix on his quarry. If it was wrong, he'd have to find out for himself, and then work out another approach.

He set off to the southwest, blazing his own trail. There was no track to follow, no guideposts, no clues. He was alone, as only solitary hunters in a vast and unfamiliar wilderness are ever truly alone.

The first muffled sound was a warning. He froze in midstride, listening. The sound was not repeated, but another followed it, distinct and different. Distinctly human. Drawing closer on a rough collision course.

Bolan had suddenly become the hunted.

MACK BOLAN ®
The Executioner

Valor is a gift. Those having it never know for sure whether they have it till the test comes. And those having it in one test never know for sure if they will have it when the next test comes.

—Carl Sandburg 1878–1967

Fear is the only language terrorists understand. As far as testing their courage goes, I'm ready to give them their final exam.

—Mack Bolan

For the troops who find themselves in harm's way
during the war on terrorism.
God keep.

Prologue

"A mighty fortress is our God…"

The voices were off-key as usual, but the Reverend Mr. Amos Claridge didn't mind. As long as they were singing, that was all that mattered. Singing in the blessed English language was twice the miracle, though Claridge reckoned he had less to do with that than others who had passed that way before him. He could tell the others hadn't been God-fearing folk, the way profanity slipped in and out of conversation with the local natives, and the poor benighted creatures didn't seem to know the difference.

"…a bulwark never failing."

Claridge raised his voice with the others, proud and strong. He wasn't the best singer himself, praise Jesus. Not even the best to graduate in his class from Trenton-Sowers Bible Institute in the year of our Lord 1975, truth be told. But he carried a tune with the best, putting muscle behind it, and wouldn't let go until the last note rang loud and clear in the breeze.

He led the hymn with gusto, loving the upturned faces ranged before him, hardly aware of their color these days, after all they'd been through together. These were his sheep—or a part of his flock, anyway, praise the Lord—and he treasured every blessed one of them.

He'd come a long way from the windswept plains of Nebraska where he'd started out on his journey of faith. A long way from clean sheets and hamburger stamped with an FDA seal of approval. Farther still from family and friends, the ones who'd stood behind him and the others who had questioned his decision.

Merilee had never questioned, never tried to change his mind, and he thanked God for that.

It was a drastic change, no doubt about it, but a call from God was rare. Few preachers ever *really* heard it, never mind what they proclaimed from pulpits or from television studios. Claridge didn't like to judge his fellow man, but he knew that some of his colleagues were lying through their polished teeth when they claimed Jesus told them to beg cash from strangers and build a new church on the rich side of town. No matter how much gospel they squeezed in between commercials, he could never trust a minister who put a price tag on the word of God.

He didn't like to judge, but Claridge knew his Bible. He was a doctor of theology as well as a pastor—it said so on the paper they had given him at Trenton-Sowers—but he couldn't abide being introduced to strangers as "Reverend Doctor." Truth be told, he wasn't all that comfortable with the "Reverend" part, since he'd always felt reverence was owed to God alone. But his sheep had to call him something, didn't they? And better "Reverend" than some things he could think of, praise the Lord.

They finished strong on the hymn, and Claridge joined in their round of applause for themselves, an odd native custom which, in his opinion, did no harm to the solemnity of the occasion.

"Good!" he said, beaming at them, spreading his arms in a gesture of embrace. "You're in fine voice today, brothers and sisters. Fine voice indeed, praise the Lord!"

"Praise the Lord!" they echoed, right on cue.

"Do we all have our Bibles?"

Thirty-seven brown hands raised their copies of the Good Book.

"Excellent!" His way was to be generous with praise and sparing with correction, when he could. "Today's lesson is about humility. Who can tell me what that means?"

A hand shot up, off to the left.

"Yes, brother?"

"The humility brings rain." All smiles, minus some teeth in front. "We have a fine humility today!"

The others nodded eagerly. "A fine humility!"

The urge to laugh almost undid him. "I believe you're thinking of *humidity,* brother. That's water in the air. *Humility* describes a quality of spirit. When we say a man is *humble,* what does that mean?"

Flat blank stares.

"It means he has no arrogance or wicked pride," Claridge explained. "He thinks of others first and places their welfare above his own—or her own, as the case may be. A humble man is *meek,* in other words. Now, Numbers 12:3 tells us that Moses was meek above all other men in the world."

Another hand went up.

"Yes, brother?"

"Pastor, me thought Moses wrote them Numbers."

"Very good! You're absolutely right, brother."

"He wrote 'em all?"

"That is correct."

"But if he tell the bloody world how meek he am, ain't that a sin of pride?"

Lord help him, they were thinking now. Claridge glanced at Merilee, sitting on the sidelines, smiling as she always did throughout each lesson. He had learned to depend on that smile in their long years together, learned to depend on her strength, but she couldn't help him now, praise Jesus.

"You'll recall, brother, that scripture is inspired by God. The sainted authors didn't just make it up as they went along. Mercy, no! They wrote as God instructed them to, don't you see?"

"God tell 'im write about how meek him is?" a woman in the front row asked.

"That's it! He works in mysterious ways, my friends."

1

Shaitan Takeri loved the jungle as an ally, trusted it to shelter him and hide his tracks from men who wanted nothing more or less from life than to exterminate him, but that didn't mean he had to love the heat, the mud and all the goddamned flies. He suffered them—along with snakes, ticks, leeches, spiders and a thousand other daily irritants—because without those things, the jungle would've been a playground and the men who hunted him would never leave until they'd tracked him down and finished it.

The jungle was his refuge, and sometimes it offered golden opportunities.

They had begun the march at dawn, knowing exactly where to find the targets. Every Sunday was the same, no matter what the season, wet or dry. The two Americans would no more miss their chance to poison native minds than they would consciously decide to give up life itself.

Fanatics were predictable. That lesson had been driven home to Shaitan Takeri, absorbed and processed. He made a point of avoiding the mistakes that led others to their doom.

They were still a few miles from the village when they met the two stragglers. Sunday-morning scoffers they would be, a pair who'd slipped away from their fellows to avoid the gathering and steal some time alone. Takeri didn't have to ask what they were doing when he saw the young man fumbling with his trousers, stooping to retrieve them, while the girl lurched to her feet, hands covering her face.

Takeri might've let them live, but the young man was stupid. Instead of simply fastening his pants, he had to be a hero, reaching for the knife that dangled from his belt. Takeri's scouts were trained to act without hesitation or remorse. One of them shot the young man in the chest before his blade had cleared its sheath.

The girl screamed out her fright and grief, but that was simply icing on the pastry. Everyone inside the village would've heard that gunshot, and for all Takeri knew, they could be scrambling to defend themselves. Seize weapons. Man the barricades.

Takeri shot the girl himself, because he was the kind of officer who led by example. His men knew better than to protest or to show any feelings as she crumpled to the ground. They had a job to do, and time was precious now.

It came down to a mad rush through the jungle, slowing only when the village was in sight. That was the time when riflemen would open fire, if they were waiting to repel invaders. But there was no gunfire, only villagers awaiting them with frightened faces, shifting nervously as if the ground had grown uncomfortably warm beneath their feet.

And then Takeri saw the targets stepping forward, standing side-by-side. They made it easy for him, when they might have run away and hidden somewhere, forcing him to search for them. It was a mark of arrogance, Takeri thought, for two unarmed Americans to think they could intimidate his men.

Today they would be proved wrong.

Takeri's men fanned out, according to the plan. He would not be surprised by lurking gunmen, wouldn't let the two Americans distract him while Death stole up behind to tap him on the shoulder.

Not today.

"Who are you?" asked the white man, standing front and center. "Why do you disturb these people?"

"You must be the preacher," Takeri said. He was thankful for a chance to use his English once again.

"I'm Reverend Amos Claridge, yes."

"And this will be your lady wife."

"I ask you once again—"

"I ask the questions here," Takeri snapped. "You answer me and otherwise be still!"

"If you expect—"

Takeri swung his AK-47 from the hip, driving its butt into the preacher's stomach, silencing his protest with a single stroke. Claridge bent double, gasping, slumping to his knees. His wife squealed like a frightened animal and knelt beside him, while the others gaped into a ring of guns.

Takeri faced the peasants and addressed them in their native language. "You are fools," he told them, "to let these outsiders fill your heads with fairy stories while the fat men in Jakarta steal the bread out of your mouths and turn your children into slaves."

Takeri stooped and plucked the dog-eared Bible from the preacher's hand, holding the book aloft. "You think this book will save you in the real world? Who believes it? Let me see your hands!"

Three hands went up immediately, clutching Bibles. Slowly, as he scanned the group, a few more arms were raised. At last, Takeri counted twelve.

"Ah, so," he said, "the twelve disciples, is it? Very good. Let's see how strong your faith is when we put it to the test."

MERILEE CLARIDGE HAD grown accustomed to hardship and doing without certain luxuries—no, make that staples—in life. She had learned to sublimate her wishes, even dreams, and to trust in her husband's interpretation of Holy Writ. That faith had served her well in their travels, at moments when she might have been afraid.

But it had not prepared her for stark raving terror.

Frozen where she knelt beside her stricken husband, she watched the gunmen from the jungle separate a dozen of their faithful students from the rest. She hadn't understood a word of what their leader said while striking Amos down, but there had been a question in it, she suspected. Twelve of the villagers had raised their hands, and now those twelve had been extracted from the group, shoved to one side. The others stood and muttered fretfully, but there was nothing they could do against so many guns.

More gunmen were returning from their quick search of the village, prodding more peasants before them. It hadn't been a perfect turnout for the Bible lesson, as it never was, but they were doing better here and in the other villages of late. Watching the new arrivals with their weapons now, she only hoped their work had not all been in vain.

The village was a small one, less than sixty full-time residents in all, so tiny in the scheme of things that it had not been named. Merilee Claridge wished it had a name, now, so that whatever the Lord allowed to happen next could be commemorated properly in prayer and song.

Too late for that. No one can hear or help us now.

The thought made her ashamed for doubting God. He knew all things, saw everyone and everything they did. Sadly, she realized, there was a universe of difference between His seeing and reaching out to help.

The Lord helps those who help themselves.

But there was nothing she could do.

She slipped an arm around her husband's shoulders, felt him trembling as he slumped beside her. Was it from the pain, she wondered, or was he afraid? What had become of all his righteous strength, just when they needed it the most?

Leaning close to him, she whispered in his ear, "We should do something, Amos!"

"Shh!" he hissed. "What can we do, but pray?"

"We can stand up, at least," she answered. Rising even as she spoke, she drew him to his feet. And wondered why he could not seem to meet her eyes.

Perhaps the action playing out before them had commanded all of his attention. Clutching one another, they stood watching as the gunmen forced their dozen prisoners to form a ragged line, standing shoulder to shoulder in the middle of the dirt track that passed for a main village street. Those chosen, self-selected as it were by the answer to some question, seemed disoriented rather than afraid. It wasn't clear to Merilee Claridge why they were singled out, or what might lie in store for them. But having seen the leading gunman's eyes, she feared the worst.

They were dead eyes, almost soulless, if such a condition could exist on God's Earth. She wondered briefly if the leader was possessed, but she had seen enough of worldly things to know that human beings on their own were capable of any evil act. They might be moved by Satan, but it didn't take a demon sitting on one shoulder to provoke another ghastly crime.

What would it be today?

Her husband muttered something, but she couldn't make it out. Bending closer, she asked him, "What, Amos? What did you say?"

"Help them…we must…."

It seemed to Merilee as if the stomach blow had reached his brain somehow, scrambling his syntax and his thoughts. How could they help the villagers against so many men with guns?

We'll pray, she thought. Clasping her husband's free hand in a fierce grip, she closed her eyes, bowed her head, and began to pray aloud. "Our Heavenly Father, hear us in this time of trial and rescue those—"

Harsh laughter grated her ears. Reluctantly, still praying, Merilee cracked her eyelids enough to see the leader of the gunmen watching her, a broad smile on his face. He half turned toward the line of villagers before him, brandishing his weapon, and barked an order at them in the singsong language of the islands. He had to repeat it, stepping closer for emphasis, before they complied. They began to speak aloud, more or less in unison. It took another moment for Merilee to sort out the jumble of their voices and understand what they were saying.

It was the Lord's Prayer.

Their captor had ordered them to pray.

Merilee stood trembling, gripping her husband's left hand hard enough to make him wince, still praying herself without any clear grasp of what words left her mouth. For all she knew, it might've been a curse. She could not stop her tongue, any more than she could force herself to step between the gunmen and her husband's poor parishioners.

They were halfway through the simple prayer. "Yea, though I walk through the valley of the shadow of death I will fear no evil, for Thou art with me…"

SHAITAN TAKERI CHOSE his moment, waited for the special words, then squeezed the trigger on his AK-47, sweeping the short line of targets from left to right. They were buckling, crumpling by the time his comrades joined in, the combined streams of automatic fire dropping some of the targets, holding others upright in a jerky dance of death, accompanied by screams from the watchers nearby.

It lasted no more than ten seconds, probably less. The last body collapsed in a heap, leaking life, while Takeri turned to face the intruders. "You see," he told them, stepping close, "your whining prayers are useless here. In this world, you have no immunity. You come with us because I say so, and you do as you are told."

"Where would you take us?" asked the white man.

"Do you want another bellyache?" Takeri sneered at him. "It's none of your concern. I take you where I wish, do with you as I please. If you are lucky, maybe someone wants you back. Maybe they pay for me to send you home."

"Ransom?"

Takeri shrugged. "Even a worn-out thing like you must have some value, yes?"

The white man smiled through bitter tears and shook his head. "You're making a mistake," he said. "The government won't pay for us. The church cannot afford—"

"Then you will die," Takeri cut him off. "When I say it is time, you join the rest and meet your Jesus, eh? But who knows, maybe you have value after all."

The white man's shoulders slumped. He faced his wife and said, "I'm sorry, Merilee. He's making a mistake. If only I—"

This time, Takeri struck him in the head. Not hard enough to crack the skull, but using force enough to put him down and guarantee a headache when the missionary shuddered back to consciousness. The wife was weeping silently, showing more strength than Takeri had seen in her man, but still pitifully weak by jungle standards. He hoped they would be ransomed soon, before they withered up and died from lack of spirit.

In the meantime...

Takeri barked orders at his men, dispersing them to scour the village and collect any objects of value they might find. He'd have to search them later, making sure they had kept nothing for themselves that would advance the movement, but he honestly expected little from a village of this size. Perhaps a little money, some food for the trail. Nothing much.

The search was necessary, all the same, just as the executions had been necessary. Normally, his men were told to treat the rural peasants with respect and try to win them over, make them allies. It was different, however, when his countrymen adopted foreign creeds and turned their backs on proud homeland traditions to please strangers. The United States of America was Shaitan Takeri's enemy. Its government supported the bastards in Jakarta and turned a blind eye to their atrocities while raiding the country's natural resources. The fat men got fatter, while ninety percent of the people toiled in abject poverty, sedated by fables of a better life that lay in store for them after they died.

Rubbish!

Takeri had no sympathy for those who willingly knuckled under to tyrants, much less those who bowed and scraped to gods imported by the very foreigners who robbed them blind and turned their children into slaves. If it required spilt blood to open up their eyes, so be it. He was equal to the task.

And if he turned a profit in the bargain, what was wrong with that?

Revolution was a risky business. Takeri placed his life on the line every day, for people he had never met and never would. Most of them didn't even know he existed. They spent their lives in dreary oblivion, serving masters who despised them, never truly dreaming of a brighter day. They would benefit from his labor all the same, and Takeri did not begrudge them that effortless gain—but neither would he harbor any needless guilt about a few brief pleasures claimed for himself along the way.

His country and his people owed him that much, at the very least.

His men were veteran looters. They would find whatever might be hidden in this place and claim it for the revolution. Later, when he had an opportunity to sift through their booty,

Takeri would decide if there was anything he wanted for himself. And none of them would argue with his judgment. They knew him far too well to take that risk.

He waited, watching the missionary's wife beside her prostrate man. She was old, maybe twice Takeri's age, and her husband older still. What had possessed them to leave their home and travel halfway around the world to this place? Did they hope to find their fortune here, or were they so deluded that they really thought their superstitious blather might improve the lot of peasants in a world they didn't understand?

Such arrogance. It made Takeri angry all over again, but he restrained himself. The prisoners should be in reasonable shape at the beginning, when demands were made. As for what happened after that... Well, that was anybody's guess.

THE NAMELESS VILLAGE had no secrets to speak of, certainly no secret hoard of wealth or weapons for the looters to uncover. By the time they finished searching, Amos Claridge had awakened to the sick pain in his head, skull cradled by his wife. Her warm tears bathed his face.

"Be still," she cautioned him. "You may be injured."

"I'll be fine," he answered, not believing it.

He stirred, regretting it at once, and rolled away from her in time to spare her from the rush of bile that stung his throat. The pain inside his head redoubled with that effort, throbbing in time to his heartbeat, bringing on another rush of nausea. When it passed, Claridge felt better, but only a little. He crawled back to Merilee on all fours, afraid to trust his legs.

There was a smell. He concentrated, breathing slowly, sorting out the acrid mixture of aromas. Gunpowder was part of it. Also the smell of bowels and bladders letting go when trauma strikes. For a heartbeat, Amos Claridge feared he might have soiled himself when he was knocked unconscious, then he realized the smell was much too strong for that—and yet removed from where he sat. There was another smell he couldn't place at first, metallic, reminding him of coins or…

Blood.

All for nothing, because a wicked fool thought Claridge and his wife had monetary value for some twisted cause. By the time their enemy learned his mistake, he would have no recourse but to kill them.

What more do I deserve? Claridge asked himself. Were not the wasted lives of his parishioners a burden on his soul? If not for him and his intrusion on their simple lives, wouldn't they be alive right now?

"My fault," he said to himself, and didn't realize that he had spoken the words aloud until Merilee answered him.

"It's not your fault," she said. "Don't even think that, Amos. You're a mighty man of God, I grant you, but you can't prevent the crimes of others when they've got machine guns and you only have the book."

"It used to be enough," he answered, softly weeping.

"Tell that to the martyrs, Amos. Were they wrong to trust in God and sacrifice themselves? He moves in mysterious ways."

"It's not my sacrifice that troubles me," he said. "These people—"

"Made their stand," she interrupted him. "They chose the Lord, and I have faith He's greeting them in Paradise right now."

"I wish I had your strength."

"You do," she said. "I've seen it countless times."

Before he could respond, the raiders came straggling back through the village, grim-faced and disgruntled from their fruitless search. Claridge struggled to his feet, dizzy, with his wife assisting him. Whatever happened next, at least he'd face it standing like a man.

The leader stood before them, smiling through any disappointment he felt at the slim pickings from the village. "It's good you're ready," he told them. "We have far to go before dark, and you mustn't slow us down."

At a snap of his fingers, two others came forward, one dangling handcuffs from his fingertips while the other unwrapped a length of rusty chain he'd worn across his chest. Claridge stood helpless as the manacles were fastened tightly on his wrists, another pair for Merilee. The chain was looped around his waist, padlocked behind, then fastened likewise to Merilee's body. A four-foot length hung slack between them, making them inseparable.

"We go now," said the leader. "Maybe you'll keep up, and I don't have to think of ways to make you march, eh?"

"I want my Bible," Claridge told him.

"Fairy tales won't help you now," the gunman said. "We go!"

The shooters shoved and prodded them until Claridge knew that any further resistance might provoke another beating. For Merilee's sake, he followed the men in front of him, trailing his captors into the jungle. He glanced back once, to find the villagers staring after him, a few still holding their Bibles before them like shields. The crumpled bodies of their fellows on the ground bore mute testimony to his failure.

And then, as the forest closed behind them, cutting off his view of the tiny settlement, the Reverend Amos Claridge heard his flock begin to sing.

"A mighty fortress is our God…"

Silently, almost hopelessly, he began to pray.

2

The aircraft was a Cessna Conquest II rigged out for jumping. That meant stripping out the passenger seats and replacing them with metal benches, nothing in the way of excess comfort for daredevils on a one-way ride. The jump bay was open, its hatch removed prior to takeoff, admitting a howl of wind and the snarl of twin turboprop engines.

It was cold at eight thousand feet, but Mack Bolan barely felt it in his insulated jumpsuit, with camouflaged jungle fatigues underneath. His pant legs were tucked into high-topped boots, and gloves covered the slight gap of sleeve at his wrists. A neoprene ski mask and goggles completed the outfit, protecting his face from the chill and rush of wind during the jump.

His gear was heavy, but nothing he hadn't carried before. Parachutes front and back were the bulk of it, two chances to do the thing right before he struck the forest canopy at three hundred miles per hour and slashed through it like a bullet through a rosebush. If both chutes failed him he was dead, and there was nothing more to say.

They wouldn't fail.

He'd never had a glitch before, and he had packed both chutes himself, as usual, under the watchful eye of a professional instructor. There was zero reason to believe that either parachute would fail to open on command. The odds against a double failure were astronomical.

Which only left the rest of it to trouble him.

The HALO jump—high altitude, low opening—would be the easy part. When Bolan set his feet on Mother Earth again, that's when his difficult mission would begin.

Unless somebody saw him coming down, of course.

In that case, they could get a fix on his position, maybe have a welcoming committee waiting for him on the ground if they were close enough. Or spare themselves the headache and spray him with auto-fire while he was still in the air.

That was the easy way to do it, and it was the reason Bolan had opted for the HALO jump. Low opening meant minimal exposure to lookouts on the ground, less time for them to chart his course and put an army underneath him, if anyone happened to see him at all.

He guessed they wouldn't, pegging the odds around seventy-thirty against being spotted. Most people didn't walk around watching the sky for no reason, especially if they were walking through jungle terrain fraught with pitfalls and dangerous wildlife. They would need a reason to look up, and that's where the HALO drop helped him again. High altitude meant less engine noise audible at ground level, less reason to glance up in search of a plane.

The jungle would help him there, too. Spotters would need a clear view of the sky, which meant piercing the forest canopy from ground level, fifty to one hundred feet below the treetops. They would need a lookout on a tower or a mountaintop to see him coming down.

Bolan recalculated the odds, making it ninety-ten that he would touch down unobserved. From that point on, however, it was anybody's game.

He got up from the bench and started toward the cockpit. In addition to the chutes, Bolan was weighted with a Steyr AUG assault rifle, a Glock 17 semiauto pistol with compact suppressor attached, multiple spare magazines for both weapons, ten fragmentation grenades, a bolo knife that doubled as tool or close-quarters weapon, a compact satellite communications outfit, an entrenching tool, two canteens filled with water, a fair-size first-aid kit and a week's worth of MRE rations. The gear didn't quite double his weight, but it was close enough for government work. Bolan felt as if he were walking underwater. He looked forward to touchdown and discarding the two bulky chutes.

The other gear, he knew, would lose weight soon enough, as he consumed the food and water, burned up ammunition and grenades. Before the game was over, he might wish he could regain some of that weight, but resupply was one more problem that he'd have to cope with on the ground.

Once Bolan jumped, he would be well and truly on his own.

Jack Grimaldi heard or felt Bolan coming and half turned in his seat to flash a smile without releasing the controls. "Ten minutes, give or take," he said, raising his voice above the wind and engine noise.

"Okay."

"All set?" Grimaldi asked.

"As ready as I'll ever be."

He ran the useless information first. The large island of Borneo was split three ways. Two-thirds of it belonged to Indonesia, and was called Kalimantan. The rest belonged to Malaysia, except for twenty-two hundred square miles on the northern coast that comprised the sovereign state of Brunei. Bolan was jumping over Kalimantan, southeast of the island's mountainous spine, where human settlements were few and far between.

That didn't mean he'd have the jungle to himself, of course.

Not even close.

He was running the important data—targets and coordinates, timetables, all the rest of it—when Grimaldi's voice cut into his concentration.

"Two minutes!"

"Right."

He slapped Grimaldi on the shoulder, gave a quick thumbs-up and walked back to the open doorway on the plane's port side. Wind rush was waiting for him, plucking at his gear and clothing, urging him to take the final step.

He couldn't hear Grimaldi now and didn't need to. Bolan had the numbers running in his head, knew well enough when it was time for him to jump. Below him, clouds concealed his target. For all he knew, there might be nothing underneath but water. He would have to pierce that veil before he could begin to navigate.

He smiled and made a leap of faith.

GRIMALDI KNEW IT WAS impossible for him to actually feel when Bolan left the plane. One human body, more or less, meant nothing to the aircraft's handling or performance. Still, he knew. He didn't have to turn and check the passenger compartment as he passed above the drop zone.

It was empty, sure as hell.

The Executioner was gone.

Grimaldi put the Cessna through a wide turn, banking gently, circling east-northeast. He would soon be over the Makassar Strait, then maybe catch himself a slice of Sulawesi as he took the bird back home to Mindanao in the Philippines. He posed no threat to anyone, maybe another tourist killing time and burning dollars, or a bush doctor making his rounds. Radar spotters might track him, but there was no reason for a radio challenge, much less a scramble of fighters. Small planes traveled here and there among the islands every day without a hitch.

Grimaldi knew the gist of Bolan's mission, but he wasn't

sure what waited for his old friend on the ground. Neither was
Bolan, if truth be told. He had a mission and a goal, but anything could happen once he dropped in from the sky. Jungle
islands were full of surprises that way, even without a hostile
reception committee, and the Indonesian archipelago held
more secrets than most. Lost tribes, perhaps, and unknown
animals. So, what was waiting for Bolan downstairs, beneath
the jungle canopy? Maybe nothing. Maybe an army. In which
case, Grimaldi almost felt sorry for the opposition.

Almost, but not quite.

His own role in the mission was distinctly limited. It was
Grimaldi's job to deliver the goods—in this case, one man—
to a selected drop at a specific time. He was, in fact, a glori-
fied delivery boy this time around. His work was finished.

But he didn't have to like it.

Bolan and Grimaldi went way back—to the beginning, really, if he looked at it a certain way. His life was going
nowhere in a hurry when he met the warrior, but Bolan had
turned it around and there'd been no looking back. Hell-bent
for leather all the way, and hardly ever a dull moment. Even
down time could be touch-and-go.

Like now.

Relaxing wasn't on Grimaldi's menu, even though he'd
done his job and had nothing more on tap until Bolan was
ready for extraction. When that time came, he wouldn't get
the word from Borneo, but rather from the U.S. military base
at Subic Bay—assuming that the satellite communication
gear Bolan was packing worked all right and didn't take a
fatal hit somewhere along the way.

If Bolan lost his voice down there, Grimaldi thought, he
just might lose it all.

Don't think that way, he warned himself. Negativity could
be addictive, and while Grimaldi didn't buy the notion that
positive thoughts determined an event's outcome, he knew

damned well from personal experience that defeatism could easily become a self-fulfilling prophecy. If he'd been on the ground with Bolan...

But that wasn't how they played the game. Grimaldi had the wings, and Bolan carried the payload. Their functions were distinct and separate. Grimaldi had spent his share of time on the firing line, but it normally came down to dogfights or strafing, kicking the hell out of ant-size targets from a thousand yards away.

Bolan's fight, by contrast, was typically up close and personal. And often, like this time, it wasn't simply a matter of finding the hostiles and taking them out. There were innocent lives on the line, and Bolan's mission was as much about extraction as it was about execution.

Sergeant Mercy, right.

It's what some of his fellow grunts had christened Bolan in another war, another lifetime. Long ago and far away that was, but the man hadn't changed where it counted. He was still a hellfire warrior and a caring soul who'd risk life limb for others without hesitation.

With Bolan, you got the whole package.

And what a package it was.

What a waste it would be if he lost it on Borneo, batting cleanup for government hacks who didn't have the *cojones* to do their own dirty work. Still, it was the kind of job that came Bolan's way all too often.

Get in, get bloody and get out.

Grimaldi did his part whenever possible, like all the rest who stand and wait to serve.

But he didn't have to like the waiting.

Not one goddamned bit.

THE FIRST RUSH OF WIND as he jumped wasn't so much a slap in the face as a punch in the gut. It was always that way on an airdrop, the first giddy rush followed up by a lurch as the wind took hold of him and shook him, showing Bolan who was boss.

Bolan struck his pose, arms back against his sides, head down. He was the classic human cannonball, hurtling through space, clouds rushing up to meet him like a solid floor. It might've made him flinch, but he'd been there and done that frequently enough to know that clouds held no menace unless they brought lightning and rain.

He'd looked at clouds from both sides, sure, and knew that their greatest threat—their greatest gift—was concealment. Jumping over unfamiliar turf, a cloud bank might hide mountain peaks, waiting to smash a jumper like a bug hitting a windshield.

Not this time, though.

He knew the ground below him well enough, from large-scale topographic maps, to understand that only treetops lay between him and impact with the ground. This time, the clouds were on his side, hiding his form a little longer from the eyes of any watchers down below. As far as radar scanners went, he was too small to raise a blip on any normal screen, much less the military surplus gear fobbed off on Third World clients by U.S. distributors.

It would be naked eyes or nothing if they saw him coming down.

The clouds wrapped Bolan in their gauzy arms for all of fifteen seconds, then he burst through into daylight once again. The island lay below him, wedge-shaped with a ragged coastal outline, mostly green where forest covered hills and valleys, hiding God knew what below their canopy.

Plummeting at seven feet per second, Bolan still had sixteen minutes and change before he had to pull the rip cord. That was time enough to scope the island from a bird's-eye view and to adjust his course by subtle body movements. He had the LZ zeroed in from aerial photos, could've stretched out an arm and pointed right to it if he'd felt like ruining his glide path.

Not a chance.

Precision was what mattered now, insertion at a point as near as possible to the exact spot chosen in advance. Every mile he veered off course would mean thirty minutes to an hour hiking through the jungle, just to reach his starting point. Bolan couldn't afford to waste that kind of time. Lives were depending on him—or they had been, when he left home base.

He only hoped that he wouldn't arrive too late.

Bolan surveyed the world below while plunging to meet it. Away to his left there was water, sun-bright and glistening like polished glass. It wouldn't help to steer in that direction if his chutes failed, since impact on water from that height would be equivalent to striking a granite slab. It was an easy way to tenderize fish food, but burial at sea wasn't on Bolan's list of things to do.

Directly under him, the island shimmered too, in darker shades of green. The slate-gray crags of mountains thrust up on his right, but Bolan would be missing those by miles, if everything worked out as planned.

Skydiving, and particularly HALO jumps, required a mixture of mental and physical preparation. An athlete could spend twenty hours a day in the gym, piling muscle on top of ripped muscle, but no amount of strength would help him if he didn't have the will, the nerve, to stand in a doorway and step into space. Conversely, the most gung-ho attitude on earth was worse than useless if it got a weak and untrained jumper killed.

Bolan had will and skill, a product of his longtime training and determination to succeed at any mission he attempted. In his world, failure wasn't simply a blow to the ego. It was the voice of Death in his ear, a razor drawn across his throat.

No one was whispering to Bolan at the moment, though. He had the sky all to himself, except for some bright-colored flecks of confetti flitting across the treetops below him, wheeling in complex maneuvers that told him they had to be birds. Bolan's LZ lay off to the left of them, but if they drifted and he had to cut through their formation, he would stick it out.

A chill had wormed its way inside his jumpsuit, but it didn't matter now. He was within two hundred feet of rip-cord time. His hand crept forward, fighting wind resistance, to find the black metal ring on his harness.

Ninety feet.

Fifty.

At zero, Bolan yanked the cord and felt the chute blossom behind him. It required another second and a half to jerk him upright, wide straps biting at his crotch and armpits, arresting his plunge toward the trees. Then he was floating instead of falling, tugging and trimming the lines to correct his angle of descent, seeking precision in a world that thrived on chaos.

He held the course, coming close to the LZ, then closed his eyes a beat before he plunged into the jungle canopy.

SERGEANT MOHAMMED SINGH had hoped for a routine patrol. If he was forced to traipse around the jungle, slapping flies and picking leeches from his skin, at least the drudgery should be completed without incident. No snakebites, no sprained ankles, none of his young soldiers straying off the trail and getting lost along the way. Above all, no rebels waiting for them in the shadows with machine guns and grenades.

This sector of the island was disputed territory, the next best thing to a free-fire zone. Leftist rebels claimed it as a "sovereign state" but couldn't stake out claims for fear of being blasted from the air. Patrols went out and sometimes came back bloodied. Some did not come back at all. The occupants of isolated forest villages were caught between the hammer and the anvil, damned by one side or the other if they demonstrated loyalty to either. Neutrality was an equally dangerous path, opening the fence-sitters to charges of disloyalty from government and rebels alike.

Singh had no intention of raiding any villages today. He had already seen enough pointless carnage to last a lifetime, and he wasn't anxious to collect more nightmare memories. Even victory left a bad taste in his mouth these days, since most of the dead were typically peasants cut down in the cross fire.

Nice and simple, Singh told himself. Out and back with nothing to report.

Behind him, the field radio made a loud crackling noise, the alert for an incoming message. Singh always flinched at that sound, well aware of how far it carried. Even if his men were expert trackers and the quietest on earth—which they most certainly were not—one blast of static from the radio would tell their enemies exactly where they were at any given time.

Singh clutched his SR-88A assault rifle more tightly. It was never good news when headquarters reached out to a squad on patrol. His superiors contacted routine patrols only in the event of some emergency. If they were ordered back to base camp, it could only mean they had an urgent, risky job to do.

Singh's corporal came forward with the radio. He offered his superior the handset, shaped like the receiver of a telephone, and said, "For you, sir."

"Yes, Singh here."

"You have new orders, Sergeant. You are to check out a report of someone falling from the sky."

Singh blinked. "Repeat please, Rajah One."

"There's no mistake, Sergeant. One of the bird-watchers reported it. A falling man, he said."

"I see." The overstatement of his week, perhaps his year.

The tinny voice of Rajah One directed him to a quarter square mile on the map Singh carried folded in his cargo pocket.

Singh handed back the radio handset and took a long step away from the corporal. The others had caught up and stood watching him, waiting.

"We have new orders," he told them. They knew it already, of course. "We march northeast from here, about four miles, to check out…something strange."

"What is it, Sergeant-sir?" one of the privates asked.

"One of the birders claims he saw a falling man," Singh answered.

For a moment they were silent, then another private asked, "Falling from where, sir?"

"Falling, I was told. You know as much as I do, now. We go and see. It's likely nothing, if a birder called it in."

Bird-watchers and stray scientists were scattered throughout Borneo and the other Indonesian islands, working on shoestring budgets from this or that international wildlife organization to find new species and identify endangered ones. In Singh's opinion, they were eccentrics for the most part, and prone to flights of fancy. Now, one of the birders had seen a man falling, and Singh was required to go look at the body.

If there was a body.

If there had ever been a falling man at all.

The best scenario would be a false alarm. No falling man, no dead or injured foreigner to carry through the jungle on the long hike back to base camp. Best case, they'd find nothing at all.

And worst case? What then? Singh didn't want to think about it. Better not to worry, after all.

The scenario, whatever it might be, would be made clear to him in time.

THE TREE HAD SNAGGED him twenty yards above the forest floor. It wasn't far to walk or run, but falling was another story altogether. Dropping sixty feet without a safety line would break his legs, at least. More likely, it would kill him outright.

Bolan dangled in his harness, glancing at the snarled chute twenty feet above his head. It was a miracle of sorts that he had missed the jutting limb before it snagged the fabric of his parachute. He wasn't sure how that had happened, and it didn't matter now. What mattered was escaping from the snare and climbing safely to the ground.

Cutting the harness was a no-go, leaving Bolan with two choices. He could either climb the tangled rigging to the limb where he was caught, or make himself a human pendulum and swing to grab the tree trunk, roughly twelve feet to his right.

He tried the climb first, muscles bunching in his arms and shoulders, straining at the nylon lines until he heard a ripping sound above him and a sudden downward lurch deprived him of the ground he'd gained. The chute's taut fabric wasn't made to hold his weight once it was snagged and torn. Another jolt or two like that, and plummeting would be the only option left.

So Bolan swung. It wasn't as easy as it sounded, starting from a stationary slump, with nothing solid to push off from. He had to gain momentum by rocking from side to side in midair, taking his time, avoiding any sudden thrusts or lunges that would make the torn chute disintegrate any faster. Twelve feet was all he needed, but it felt like half a mile to Bolan, picking up an inch or two on each slow arc above the yawning chasm of the jungle floor.

He picked up speed by slow degrees, tensing against the moment when the chute would come apart. When that happened, Bolan's survival would depend upon the laws of physics. If it caught him anywhere except the long arc toward the tree, free fall and shattered bones awaited him. If he could grasp the trunk before his chute gave way, he had a decent chance to save himself.

He swung out and back, out and back, almost reluctant to breathe in case the extra weight of fresh air in his lungs should prove too much for the strained fabric sling overhead.

He felt the chute going before he heard it, sensed a slackening in the lines that held him dangling sixty feet above the ground. It parted on the backswing, gravity asserting its claim while centrifugal force fought back. He was falling and swinging, all at the same time, arms outstretched to grasp whatever slender hope remained.

The first branch couldn't hold him. Bolan grabbed it, grunting as it snapped off in his hands and let him drop. He clawed the tree's rough bark in vain, then snagged another limb beneath his left arm, striking almost hard enough to dislocate his shoulder.

But it held.

Bolan took a moment to regain his equilibrium and catch his breath. That done, he wriggled free of the parachute harness and pushed it away. He wouldn't be able to bury the gear but, by the time anyone came around, looking twenty yards up from the ground, he should be well away.

Time to climb.

It was treacherous going, smooth bark under the soles of his boots refusing solid purchase, but there were enough strong branches to permit awkward progress. They ran out twenty feet above the ground, but that was fine. Dangling by his hands from the last limb he trusted, Bolan's feet were only twelve feet or so from the ground. He dropped without injury, landing in a practiced crouch.

The earth felt alien beneath his feet, after the flight, the long drop and his scrambling climb. Walking felt strange, but only for the first half-dozen steps. By then, Bolan had unlimbered his Steyr AUG and he was ready to rock at the first sign of danger.

He checked his wrist compass and plotted a course in his mind. He couldn't be sure if the target was where he'd been told it would be. Things changed, day to day, and his intelligence might've been faulty to start with. Still, it was the only lead he had, the only fix on his quarry. If it was wrong, he'd have to find out for himself and then work out another approach.

Bolan set off to the southwest, blazing his own trail as he went. There was no track to follow, no guideposts, no clues. He was alone, as only solitary hunters in a vast and unfamiliar wilderness are every truly alone.

Or, was he?

The first muffled sound was a warning. He froze in midstride, listening. The sound was not repeated, but another followed it, distinct and different.

Distinctly human.

Drawing closer on a rough collision course.

Bolan had suddenly become the hunted.

There was someone on his trail.

3

Two days before the HALO jump, Bolan had walked among the silent dead at Arlington. All those interred within that hallowed ground had served their country during times of need. Some had been recognized as heroes while in uniform, or as they fell on blood-drenched battlefields. Others, like Medgar Evers, found a sacred cause after they shed their uniforms and sacrificed themselves in its pursuit. And, human nature being what it is, Bolan guessed that some of them could not bear close examination without tarnishing distorted memories.

A human rainbow lay beneath the cemetery's snow-white monuments and neatly manicured grass. Bolan supposed the only thing they had in common was that they were dead and gone.

But not forgotten.

He had to believe that everything counted, somehow.

Why else had he answered the call?

This one had come, as they so often did, from Hal Brognola. On paper, Brognola was one of the Justice Department's key management figures. In fact, he'd been handpicked by a former White House resident to oversee the covert operations run from Stony Man Farm, nestled in the Blue Ridge Mountains of Virginia. The mere fact that he'd survived successive presidents, with their varied agendas and temperaments, spoke volumes about Brognola's efficiency.

He was the best at what he did, bar none.

And when he said a job was urgent, Bolan took him at his word.

Bolan had long since given up on trying to second-guess Brognola. Once upon a time, he might've linked the timing of a call to some event reported by the media, perhaps surmising where his next campaign would be fought. These days, however, planet Earth was in such ever-changing turmoil that he didn't waste the time on guessing games.

A shadow fell across the grave marker in front of him. He waited for the gruff, familiar voice.

"You're right on time, as usual," Brognola said.

"You called it urgent," Bolan said. His handshake was a warm vice grip. Brognola tried to match it, grateful that the big guy didn't feel a need to prove himself by grinding knuckles.

"Urgent sums it up," Brognola replied. "Let's take a walk."

He didn't take the same comfort from Arlington that Bolan seemed to find in their occasional graveyard meetings. For Brognola, the place seemed less about victory than loss.

"You heard about the missionaries that were snatched last week?" he asked, breaking the ice.

"Borneo, wasn't it?" Bolan queried.

"Reverend Amos Claridge and his wife Merilee," Brognola went on. "They're members of some offshoot Southern Baptist splinter sect, about as fundamental as it gets. They got a call from the Almighty some time back, apparently. Gave up their stateside church and went to save some Third World heathens."

"Okay. And now these two are in the bag," Bolan said.

"Big time," Brognola replied. "Our embassy in Manila got a message from the kidnappers, day before yesterday. It's an outfit called the Sword of Freedom. Ever heard of them?"

"Maoist guerrillas, at least on paper," Bolan answered from memory. "They've been staging sporadic antigovernment attacks for the past three or four years, unless I've mixed them up with someone else."

"You haven't," Brognola assured him. "They're not the largest group of Indonesian insurgents, but they're among the most active right now. And they've got our attention with this job, right up to the top."

"What's being done to spring the hostages?"

"The usual. Jakarta hasn't been able to get a handle on this outfit since it started lighting fuses. They send out patrols and hassle native 'suspects,' throw a few more urban dissidents in jail and call it a day. This time, we're afraid they may do more."

"How's that?" asked Bolan.

"You remember that mess in the Philippines, a few years ago?"

"Another missionary couple," Bolan said. "The Philippine army found them, but they had some problems."

"That's the understatement of the year," Brognola replied. "In fact, they killed the husband and a couple of other hostages, then tried to blame it on the rebels. Ballistics made the case, but no one followed up officially."

"It sounds familiar," Bolan said grimly.

"It would be incorrect to say that no one took a hit on that deal, though. The White House got letters, lots of them, and Congress got more. The House wanted to pass a resolution, but it fell a few votes short. The couple's church tried to sue the Philippine government, but Justice talked them out of it."

"And that's important…why?" Bolan asked.

"Long story short," Brognola said, "nobody wants an instant replay of the first fiasco. The word from on high is that we *must not* have another snafu of that kind."

"So you want them extracted, intact."

"That's the ticket. No harm, no foul. And no strained relations with our friends in Jakarta."

"They won't know I'm coming." Bolan didn't make it sound like a question.

"Wouldn't be prudent," Brognola replied. "We don't want to step on any toes, imply they're less than competent."

"Extraction's all you want, or is it search and destroy?"

"Your option. I assume there'll be some contact with the snatch team during extrication, but it's not our primary concern. Whatever happens, do what you have to do."

"It could get dicey with the locals."

Brognola knew he meant the Indonesian military and police. "I won't deny you may run into someone, once you're in the bush," Brognola said. "Jakarta says they're looking, doing everything they can to save the hostages. You know the drill. I can't promise you won't run into a patrol or three, before you're done."

"That leaves the targets," Bolan said. "Last time I scoped an atlas, Borneo was bigger than Texas. I can't just wander around and hope I get lucky."

"We've done some homework, as you may imagine," Brognola answered. "Between informants and satellite surveillance, we've got a fair fix on the Sword of Freedom's home base."

"How fair?"

"Eighty-five percent confidence," Brognola said.

It wasn't bad, as educated guesses went. That wouldn't help, of course, if they turned out to be dead wrong. Pinpoint insertion on a worthless target would accomplish nothing.

"Ground contacts?" Bolan asked.

"Not this time," Brognola said. "There are informants, as I said, but they won't go the extra mile and lead a strike against the Sword. Too much to lose."

"When do I take off?"

"I've got Grimaldi standing by, and hardware's waiting for you at the other end. You'll be in contact via satellite for the extraction."

"If and when," said Bolan.

"When, not if."

"It's never cut and dried," the Executioner reminded him.

At what would be his final destination, it was already the next day.

Bolan wondered if he'd be in time to help the hostages, or if he'd even find them on the huge, thickly forested island. Brognola seemed confident on that score, and his intelligence rarely disappointed Bolan, but there were still too many wild cards in the game to make it a sure thing.

For starters, Bolan's enemies were volatile and unpredictable. The Sword of Freedom was a rural outfit, for the most part, but over the past twelve months it had claimed responsibility for half a dozen car bombings in Jakarta and Palembang, rocking government facilities and claiming multiple lives. The group was strongest in Kalimantan, where its spokesmen called for independence and the establishment of a vaguely defined socialist state. Bolan wondered if their program was a front for something else, but that was beyond the scope of his mission at the moment.

His second problem was the Indonesian government itself. The military was a rough-and-ready crew with few regards for human rights. They'd demonstrated that with periodic massacres that dated back to 1965, more recently with actions in East Timor that United Nations peacekeepers described as genocide. His problem with the locals was their propensity for using random brute force over strategy, preferring punishment to rescue.

And rescue, this time, was the name of the game.

Which brought him to his third problem: the hostages themselves. He didn't know the Claridges, but Bolan understood that missionaries were human beings, which meant they acted from the same variety of motives common to all other members of their species. Religion was a means of defining character, but it was only one means. In his time, Bolan had known preachers who ranged from virtual saints to the dregs of society, and everything in between. He believed, until proved wrong on an individual basis, that most were sincere in their wish to be helpful—whatever that meant in their particular creeds. Even then, however, private quirks in personality determined whether any given missionary was a more- or less-desirable hostage.

Some preachers were calm, beatific, patient to a fault. Others were imperious, demanding, confrontational. One might survive captivity more or less unscathed, while another could provoke his captors into deadly violence with a show of arrogant superiority.

It took all kinds, but not all kinds survived.

The wife could be a separate problem, in and of herself. Female hostages were always doubly at risk with male captors, though age, appearance and personal demeanor typically affected the likelihood of sexual assault. Bolan did not subscribe to the belief that women were a "weaker" sex, except to the extent that sheer size or physical power affected performance of specific tasks. Still, in his professional opinion, a middle-aged housewife from the American Midwest was less likely to emerge intact from prolonged jungle captivity than most healthy men in the same situation.

The other wild cards in the deck included everything from weather and wildlife to disease, freak accidents, and the temperament of native villagers who interacted with the Sword of Freedom rebels. Were the kidnappers popular heroes, or were they feared and despised? Had the Claridges converted any followers who might attempt to free them independently?

Wild cards. By definition, they showed up when least expected. What a player made of them depended on his own skill, personality and nerve. Incipient disaster might turn out to be a saving grace, if handled properly. By the same token, lucky breaks could wind up baiting lethal traps.

Bolan had an above-average record for hostage extrication, no question about it. Any hostage negotiator would've envied his stats, though negotiation had little to do with Bolan's particular style. By the same token, he'd lost his share of comrades and captives under fire, and every one of them was fresh in his mind.

Bolan didn't blame himself, per se, for losing hostages. Murderers bore responsibility for their own actions, but he tried to learn from every losing situation and improve his technique the next time around.

And the one certainty in Bolan's experience was that there would be a next time.

4

There was someone on his trail.

Bolan couldn't tell how many people were approaching, but he made it plural from the racket they produced. One man, if concentrating, could be fairly quiet in the forest, though the kind of silence imagined by fiction writers was rarely achieved in nature—and on those occasions when it was, the very lack of background noise became an automatic danger warning.

Movement equaled sound, unless the subject had been sucked into a sterile vacuum, and the jungle offered several dozen opportunities for rustling, sliding, snapping sounds each time a hunter took a step. The best knew that and made allowances. The worst blundered ahead, as if they had the wide world to themselves.

The men on Bolan's trail fell somewhere between the two extremes.

He had a choice to make, and quickly: flight or fight?

Both options came with risks attached. Fleeing, he would be forced to make some hasty noises of his own, and there was no guarantee he could outrun the hunters or find a secure hiding place without more time for searching. If he fought, Bolan might find himself outgunned and overmatched, but even if he won and took down the trackers, it meant the end of anything resembling a soft probe on Borneo.

What difference did that make, if they were after him already? Then again, what if they weren't? What if the noise he heard was made by native hunters, or a squad of soldiers out on a routine patrol? There was no reason to assume they had come hunting him specifically, but it was safer if he played the game that way and left nothing to chance.

There were two things that he absolutely couldn't do. The first was meet these strangers with a smile and a wave in the middle of nowhere, asking them for directions to the nearest rebel campsite.

The other was waste one more second of time.

He melted into the jungle, retreating on an oblique angle from the hunters' line of march, making no more noise than necessary. He was covered on that end, to some extent, because the new arrivals wouldn't hear much above their own racket, unless shots were fired.

This was the reason he'd chosen the Glock 17 with suppressor attached. The weapon would fire in almost any condition—frozen, muddy, under water—and the suppressor mounted on its muzzle would make the subsonic 9 mm Parabellum rounds nearly silent. They'd be quiet enough, at any rate, to grant him the advantage of surprise.

Ideally, Bolan wanted to avoid contact. He had a destination, map coordinates, the whole nine yards, but he might never get to use them if the mission blew up in his face before he'd spent an hour on the ground. He reckoned this was either bad luck squared, or evidence that somebody had seen him coming down.

He heard them talking now, a couple of the point men making noise to stay in touch or calm their nerves. Whatever they were thinking, it was careless, could've got them killed. It might still get them killed, if Bolan couldn't get out of their path or find a decent refuge for himself.

From the sound of it, he gathered they were fanning out.

The Executioner®
Don Pendleton's

HOUR OF JUDGMENT

A GOLD EAGLE BOOK FROM

WORLDWIDE®

TORONTO • NEW YORK • LONDON
AMSTERDAM • PARIS • SYDNEY • HAMBURG
STOCKHOLM • ATHENS • TOKYO • MILAN
MADRID • WARSAW • BUDAPEST • AUCKLAND

First edition April 2005
ISBN 0-373-64317-9

Special thanks and acknowledgment to
Michael Newton for his contribution to this work.

HOUR OF JUDGMENT

Printed in U.S.A.

No point to that, unless they planned a search for something in the area. Bolan had never been a great believer in coincidence, although he knew things happened just by chance from time to time. It was a stretch, though to believe a hunting party would appear from nowhere at that moment, and begin to sweep his drop zone, if they weren't looking specifically for him.

Your basic snowball would get better odds in Hell.

So, they were hunting him—or a jumper who'd been spotted by one of those witnesses Bolan had hoped would not be glancing skyward when he hit the silk. Someone had seen the chute, and now he had a quick-response team on his trail, but they still didn't have a fix on him.

Not yet.

He took for granted that their knowledge of local terrain surpassed his own. For all his topographic maps and photos, all the homework he had done, Bolan was still a drop-in. There was no way he could equal native knowledge of the ground, and thus no certain way for him to outrun the patrol.

Forget flight, then.

Now it was *hide* or fight.

The hunters had fanned out into a skirmish line, sweeping the bush, and so improved the odds that they would find him on the ground. He couldn't burrow deep enough to lose them in the time allotted him, which only left one option.

It was time to climb.

He didn't like it, and he might've come up with a better notion, given time to think. But time was one more thing he didn't have. The longer he stood searching for alternatives, the closer came his enemies.

Bolan picked out a tree with branches low enough to get him started, foliage thick enough to cover him, and a fair field of fire in case push came to shove. His boots scuffed the trunk going up, no way to avoid it, and then he was climbing, hoping the hunters weren't woodsmen enough to follow his footprints and scratches on bark.

If they were, he was probably dead. Being treed was a definite worst-case scenario, sure, but at least he could put up a fight. Before they knocked him from his perch, some forty feet above the ground, Bolan could pepper them with rifle fire and frag grenades, take out a few of them to keep him company.

He didn't need the Glock, now. If they spied him in the tree, or simply started firing blindly through the foliage, he would need the Steyr's firepower, and no suppressor was required.

Clutching a limb with one hand and his weapon with the other, Bolan settled in to wait.

SERGEANT MOHAMMED SINGH was troubled. They'd found no traces of the so-called falling man, so far, but instinct told him there was something wrong, and he couldn't rest until he found out what it was.

The easy route would be to blame it on the birder. All of them were known to be prone to exaggeration if not outright fabrication. Singh could spend another hour searching, then head back to base camp and report that there was nothing to be seen.

But what if he was wrong?

Eighteen years in uniform had taught him that most patrols were make-work assignments, dispatched without much hope of enemy contact. Lately, however, his superiors had been highly agitated by rebel activity in Kalimantan, and especially by the abduction of two meddling American do-gooders. They were worse than the birders, this lot, always poking their noses into someone else's business, telling their reluctant hosts how to lead their lives.

Singh wouldn't miss them, but it would look bad for

Jakarta if the army couldn't keep the peace and rescue those two from the clutches of guerrillas. It emboldened rebels and annoyed the government's free-spending friends in Washington. It would be a feather in Singh's turban if he found the missing couple, but that wasn't why he'd been sent to this particular patch of jungle.

Where was the falling man? Did he even exist?

"Sergeant-sir!"

Singh grimaced at the shout. His men made noise enough to wake the dead. "What is it, Private?"

"There's a footprint, sir."

"What kind of footprint, Private?"

"Sir, a *foot*print!"

Singh moved to his left, and brushed past two soldiers more or less at ease, to reach the one who'd called him. Overhead and all around, the forest had gone still in response to their voices.

"Where is it?" Singh demanded.

"There, sir!"

Young and nervous, not quite smiling, the private pointed to a semicircular smudge in the mud. Singh crouched to study it. He thought it might've been a print from someone's boot heel, with the tread smudged, or it could've been a mark from a large animal. Singh looked for other marks, found none and scowled.

It might be nothing, but he couldn't take that chance.

"How does a falling man leave one footprint, then disappear?" he asked.

"I don't know, Sergeant-sir," the private said.

"I don't know either, Private."

To the squad at large, he called out, "Sharp eyes now! We may have one man moving south. Report whatever signs are visible."

Within five minutes, Singh regretted that order. The first

call brought him to inspect a broken twig. The next revealed
a pile of droppings that he took to be a forest hog's. Another
showed him scratches on a tree trunk, where a cat had paused
to stretch and mark its territory. Yet another led him to a bed
of ferns, mashed flat by the application of some unknown
weight.

Nothing and more nothing.

For all those scattered signs to speak of human passage,
Singh had to believe a troupe of soldiers larger than his own
had gone before him, not in columns, but spread out across
a front nearly one hundred yards wide. One falling man had
thus become a veritable marching band. It was impossible.

And yet...

What if the birder *had* seen something? Someone?

"Falling" could mean jumping from an airplane. People
did it all the time, around the world.

But not on Borneo.

A parachutist on the island—more particularly in this sector of the island—would not be a daredevil in search of thrills.
There would be purpose to a stunt like that, and while Singh
couldn't work out what that purpose may have been, he understood that it was almost certainly forbidden by the state.

Jakarta would've warned his superiors if an airborne op-
eration was planned for this sector, even if it was merely a
field exercise. Covert jumpers meant trouble, and all the more
credit to whoever bagged one.

If he existed.

Because he might, Singh did not reprimand his men for
pointing out overturned stones and smudge marks on logs. It
only took one proper clue, a little bit of luck, to put him on
the trail.

Promotion could be his, perhaps a decoration, if they were
successful. It would hardly matter which of Singh's soldiers
first glimpsed the prey, since he was in command and all the

credit thus belonged to him. Likewise, of course, he would be saddled with responsibility if they should fail.

The only punishable failure would occur if they observed an enemy, then let him slip away. If they found nothing in the jungle, he could always blame it on the birder's wild imagination.

"Sharp eyes!" Singh called out to them again. "Remember why we're here."

BOLAN TRACKED HIS pursuers by their sounds. He couldn't see them through the screen of leaves, meaning that they couldn't see him either. It was the rule of hide-and-seek, as true in combat as in childhood play, although the stakes had changed.

He caught his breath when the hunters paused beneath his tree, wishing he could understand their muttered conversation. Had they spotted marks that betrayed his climb? If so, would they send someone up to find him, or stand back and spray the tree with automatic fire?

Bolan knew he was getting ahead of himself, since he hadn't glimpsed the trackers yet and couldn't swear that they were soldiers. Still, they had the military sound about them, boots on turf, the shifting noise of gear and weapons that hadn't been taped and secured to permit near-silent passage.

Soldiers, then. But for which side?

They could be government troops, or members of the very rebel group he sought. In either case, the contact would be premature. He needed time to check out the coordinates Brognola's intel had provided, cover the ground on his own and find out if the hostages were caged where he expected them to be.

Contact with either side was not a part of Bolan's plan. Whichever group was sniffing down below him, he needed to avoid discovery for the moment. And if that meant taking out unlucky witnesses, so be it.

He'd thought about the Indonesian military, the atrocities those troops had carried out, and he'd decided that his private ban on using deadly force against police did not extend to every storm trooper in uniform. Many troops were nothing more than thugs with a regular paycheck, commanded by gangsters with medals pinned on their jackets. Granted, they were thugs and gangsters with a rubber-stamp seal of approval from Congress, but Bolan had not been dispatched on a goodwill mission.

He was there to extricate specific prisoners, and to do it without fail. Anyone who opposed him was gambling with fate.

The searchers moved on. Whatever they'd found at the base of Bolan's tree, it hadn't intrigued them enough to look further. They retreated slowly, toward the south, with one calling out instructions of some kind to the others. Again, Bolan wished for a translator, knowing he'd have to make do without one.

Waiting in the tree, his index finger crooked around the Steyr's trigger and the rifle set for full-auto-fire, Bolan imagined what might be happening below him. The retreat could be a trick, of course. They could have sentries posted on the ground, waiting and watching while the others made a show of moving on. In that case, Bolan wouldn't know until he started climbing down, unless the lookouts should do something stupid. Lighting cigarettes, blowing their noses, coughing, whispering among themselves.

But it was quiet on the ground. He smelled no odor of tobacco, picked up nothing that would tell him men were waiting down below to blast him from his perch.

Bolan waited, timing his move, trying to judge when it was safest to descend.

He'd give them five more minutes, then climb down. If there were sentries waiting for him on the ground, so be it.

Bolan had ticked off ninety seconds in his head, when a commotion erupted in the forest northeast of his perch. He didn't hear the initial disturbance, but someone gave a warning shout he couldn't understand, and then the search party went crashing off through the forest like a stampeding herd of buffalo.

It didn't sound as if they were pursued, more like the hunters had been chasing someone through the jungle. Bolan didn't know what that was all about, but he started the five-minute countdown over from scratch while he listened to the fading sounds of pursuit.

He descended slowly from his perch, the rifle slung across his back once more. This was the vulnerable time, when shooters on the ground could pick him off before he had a chance to reach the Glock or one of his grenades. The sole alternative was jumping, but it wouldn't grant him any real advantage, and he didn't care to risk a twisted ankle on the first day of his mission.

His worst moment, breaking through the leaves, came seconds later. At that juncture, any ambush party would see Bolan coming down the tree feetfirst, hands occupied, before he had a glimpse of them. It was the perfect killing time—but nothing happened.

Bolan dropped the last ten feet and had the Steyr in his hands before he hit the fighting crouch. Around him, he saw nothing more sinister than ferns and creepers, vying for meager sunlight a hundred feet below the forest canopy. Footprints betrayed the presence of the hunters who had treed him, but they'd left no other traces of themselves.

He could've followed them, but they were going in the wrong direction and it would've meant more wasted time. The last thing Bolan needed at the moment was a pointless detour to nowhere. Bolan was heading off to the southwest, and he had miles to go before he slept.

Assuming he got any sleep at all.

THE RUNNER BROKE contact with his pursuers once they had a fixed direction and were making decent time. He didn't need to lead them any farther north, as long as they were moving on their own incentive, and his business lay in the other direction.

He wanted a look at the one they'd been hunting, before the man slipped out of range.

The soldiers had taken his bait without question or hesitation, plunging headlong in pursuit as soon as they picked up the careless noise of his flight. They were programmed to fight guerrillas, untutored in tactics, and they'd thrown discretion to the wind without a second thought.

He could've killed them then, there weren't that many, but it wasn't in the plan. Evasion was enough for now, and if he had to kill them later, or some others like them, he would deal with that in time.

Ditching the soldiers wasn't any great achievement. All he had to do was get them started, then conceal himself and let the party pass him by, gaining momentum as it went. He guessed they'd cover a kilometer or more before they understood that something had gone wrong, and by the time they doubled back—if they decided it was worth the time and effort—he would be long gone. The trick was locating a decent hideout in a hurry, and he'd taken his cue from the man he'd been stalking when the soldiers interrupted.

If in doubt, seek altitude.

He'd grabbed a long vine on the run and trusted it to hold his weight, scrambling aloft in seconds flat. The vine had been a dicey gamble, but it hadn't dropped him on his ass in front of his pursuers. It held. Whatever noise he made was lost in the cacophony the hunters raised, behind him.

He'd been watching when they passed beneath him, ready with his finger on the trigger of his CAR-15, but there'd been no call for a strafing run. He saved his ammunition for the main event and watched the seekers pass from sight before he dropped back to the ground.

The clock was running, and he felt it.

He had no idea who the lone prowler was, but he meant to find out. From what little he'd seen, the guy wasn't native. A white man, for sure, but that left all of Europe, as well as North America and Australia. Their missions might be unrelated, but the runner needed leads. He couldn't let a possibility slip through his hands before it was explored, examined and rejected.

Retracing his stealthy path through the jungle, he ran through a short list of possibilities. The treed man could be some kind of merc, but that left the question of who had employed him, and why. He wasn't an adviser to the local military, that was obvious. What else could be?

A rebel?

No. Whatever else he might be, this guy wasn't native, and Indonesian guerrillas weren't known for importing hired help.

Some kind of big-game hunter?

No, again. The gear was wrong, and hunters paid big bucks these days to stalk Third World wildlife, complete with official permits.

Some kind of criminal or smuggler?

Maybe. But what was his business out here in the middle of nowhere, and why had he come on his own?

The runner couldn't think of any other options at the moment, but he trusted observation to fill in some of the gaps.

Of course, he had to catch up with the treed man first, before he could observe, and simple logic told him the guy should be grounded and moving by now. He was too slick and sly to wait forever in that tree. Whatever business brought him to this place, he wouldn't want to put it off a moment longer than was absolutely necessary.

No one came to Borneo's worst jungle on vacation.

I'll find out soon enough, the runner thought.

But he would have to watch himself a bit more closely. Snap judgments of a total stranger's character were always risky, but he'd glimpsed this one in action and could say without fear of contradiction that the guy was some kind of pro. As to what kind, well, that was still anyone's guess.

Don't make assumptions, the runner cautioned himself. That was a cardinal mistake in combat situations. It led soldiers astray, blurred their vision and could be as deadly in its way as reckless overconfidence or rank defeatism. Reality was all that mattered on a battlefield, and he was still scoping out the three-dimensional reality of his present situation.

Putting it together one piece at a time.

He was close now. His troop of pursuers had left ample signs of their passage for any trained woodsman to follow, and the runner knew he was near the point where he'd foxed them into their stampede. Another few yards, and he'd be looking at the tree where his quarry had hidden and let them pass by. From there, he'd have to scout the ground and see which way the man had gone, but that should be no challenge.

The runner had been hunting all his life. His father had approved of it, sending the message of mankind's dominion over beasts, and for the past few years he'd studied the techniques of following two-legged game. It seemed, now, that his life had all been channeled toward this moment and the moments that would follow, schooling him for what he'd have to do.

Thy will be done.

Amen.

Emerging from the shrubbery, he started scouting for the solitary stranger's signs.

BOLAN HAD COVERED LESS than a hundred yards when he realized that he was being followed. Again. It wasn't like last time, with the casual, almost reckless advance of men too bored or weary to care if they set off alarms.

This time the hunter knew what he was doing and was taking time to get it right. One man, or maybe two, but definitely not a squad of ground-pounders with time to kill and nowhere special to go.

A different species of professional, thus doubly dangerous.

There were two ways to deal with a stalker: ditch him or take him out. The arguments against evasion were the same with one or two hunters as they had been earlier, with the noisy troop of soldiers. Unfamiliar ground was a handicap, and Bolan had to assume that his adversary knew the ground better, might have been raised to know every game trail.

Long-term evasion was likely a losing proposition, then. A time waster and energy consumer that would probably yield no worthwhile results.

Take him out.

That option came with problems of its own. At any other time, he could've risked an ambush from a distance, dropped his adversary with a rifle shot and left him on the trail to feed the jungle scavengers. This time, however, any untoward noise could bring the soldiers racing back from whatever wild errand had distracted them the first time. That, in turn, would mean a fresh pursuit, and probably a running firefight through the forest. In the process, his pursuers might have time to radio for reinforcements.

If he followed that scenario to its conclusion, Bolan's mission could be scuttled on day one, before he ever had a chance to see his target, much less extricate the hostages. It was the worst-case, squared.

No good.

A quiet confrontation, then. He needed to surprise the stalker, catch him unaware and use his blade or quiet Glock before the enemy could raise a fuss and draw attention from the home team. Two stalkers would make it doubly difficult, but not impossible.

The first thing he needed was someplace to hide. A quick scan showed him no cover of substance within easy reach. The forest undergrowth might hide him from a casual inspection, but it wouldn't stop bullets or provide true concealment. To surprise his stalker, Bolan needed both a hiding place and launching pad.

Go high, he thought, and for the second time in as many hours he looked for a convenient tree.

There was no shortage in the forest, and he chose one with branches that hung over the vestige of a trail that he'd been following. Since the stalker was behind him, Bolan climbed the south side of the tree, thereby concealing any scuff marks from approaching eyes. Before his adversary had a chance to circle the trunk and inspect it, Bolan hoped to have him down and out.

Well, down, at least.

He didn't want to kill the man or men on sight, unless a single glimpse convinced him they were mortal enemies. Leaving a trail of bodies in his wake was not the surest way to pass unnoticed, but Bolan could always hide them if it came to that.

First, though, he wanted to see the stalker's eyes.

Patience was a sniper's virtue, but everyone had nerves, anxiety of some kind. Crouching in the tree, hands empty, waiting to decide which weapon he should use, Bolan felt a certain curiosity regarding his opponent.

This was no random contact, as the first had been. He wasn't simply standing in the way of some routine patrol passing through. This time, he was clearly the target.

But whose?

It wouldn't be long, now, until he found out.

The subtle sounds came closer. There was nothing that the

average hiker would notice, but Bolan had never been average. He'd lived as long as he had through a painstaking attention to detail in every move he made, particularly when he trespassed on the killing grounds.

Footsteps, however cautiously placed, still left aural and physical traces. A body brushing through undergrowth might take its time and avoid slapping limbs, but it still had to move, or the hunt was aborted. Progress meant motion, and motion meant disturbance of the atmosphere, however slight.

It took a skilled hunter of humans to pick up the signs, and Bolan had more time invested in that profession than most opponents he met in the course of a mission. Those who could match his talent and experience were very few and very far between.

Would this be one of them?

He didn't think so, but he kept an open mind.

No expectations meant no rude surprises. No upsets.

No knife in the back.

Bolan waited. Moments later, a man in camouflage fatigues and facial paint came into view. The stalker hesitated before leaving cover, then crept forward, following the trail. Bolan observed his gear and saw that his head weapon was a U.S.-manufactured CAR-15, the carbine version of the classic M-16.

In a country whose military was supplied primarily by the United States, that could mean anything, or nothing. Bolan let it go and braced himself.

The stalker came closer, step by cautious step. Another moment placed him under Bolan's tree.

Just one more yard...

Without a hint of warning, Bolan fell upon him like the wrath of God.

5

The stalker had a heartbeat's warning and half turned in his crouching stance. Then the full weight of a plummeting two hundred pound body drove him to the ground with stunning force. He lost the CAR-15, there was no way to keep his grip on it despite his training. The air rushed from his lungs and left him feeling like a stranded fish.

But he fought back.

A raw survival instinct overrode the shock and numbing force of impact from above. No matter if he felt as if he were drowning on dry land, there was an enemy on top of him who had to go or there'd be no tomorrow.

Fighting for survival entailed both training and reflex. He'd studied the moves until they were like second nature, but some of them fled his mind now, when it came to the crunch. At the same time, he knew a man's weak points from lifelong experience, knew where to probe, pinch and strike for the maximum painful effect.

His enemy knew the points, too.

The stalker blocked a roundhouse to the head and grimaced as a short jab found his kidney. He wheezed painfully through clenched teeth. He didn't have the breath to spare for cursing, so the fight was silent, desperate. He kicked out with his boots but punished only air. An elbow slammed into his ribs, retreated, then came back to set off fireworks in his skull.

God help me!

With a frantic heave and roll, he pitched the stranger off and rolled a few yards toward the tree from which his enemy had dropped. Lurching to hands and knees, the stalker half rolled, braced his spine against the trunk and levered with his trembling legs to come erect.

What he saw confirmed the stalker's early estimation. Mr. X was tall, well built and plenty strong. His jungle gear could've been plucked from any military-surplus store between New York and Sydney. He was tough and fit.

And at the moment, he was winning.

The stalker drew a ragged breath.

The big man rushed him, feinting with a left, sidestepping the defensive high kick, and striking low to the back with his right. The damned kidney again, and a bright lance of pain pierced the stalker, wringing an involuntary cry from his throat.

Bad sign. A show of weakness.

Compensating, he lashed out with feet and fists, striking his adversary on an upraised arm, bruising the leg that blocked his groin kick. In return, he caught a straight-arm to the chest that drove him back against the tree. Its trunk was all that kept him from collapsing as he fought for breath once more.

Time to get serious.

He slumped, his right arm dangling, while the left shielded his bruised rib cage, trying to look as if the kick had stunned him. His right hand found the boot knife in an instant, drew it, and the six-inch blade was ready to deflate his adversary's charge.

It never came.

Instead of rushing in, the big guy took a backward step and drew a long knife of his own. Some kind of bolo, with a heavy blade and curved cutting edge, designed to cut through shrubbery or flesh and bone with equal ease.

Now, that's a knife, the stalker thought, and recognized the hard edge of hysteria in the laughter that rose to his throat.

He choked it down and stepped off from the tree, circling in a classic knife-fighter's crouch.

"Be sure you want to do this," said the other man.

English.

What else had he expected? Halfway around the world from home, he'd seen this character appear from nowhere, in the middle of the jungle, and had guessed the guy might have some information that would help him on his way. Under other circumstances, maybe they'd have shared a beer and had a simple conversation, but it surely wasn't working out that way.

"Be sure," the stranger said again.

There were two ways to play it. Strong and silent, going for the jugular, or stringing him along until he found an opening and made his move. The stalker saw no great advantage, either way, and so he kept his mouth shut.

Circling.

The movement took him counterclockwise, with his opposition mirroring each step. There would be no advantage for either side, until one of them made a critical mistake.

Who would it be?

Most likely, whoever had taken more hits and sustained more damage. That put him at a disadvantage.

Despite his training, mental preparation and the rest of it, he'd never killed a man before. If he survived this confrontation, it would be a first, but God knew he was motivated to succeed.

The spirit's willing, but the flesh is weak.

He'd come a long way to be gutted by a stranger, with his righteous mission barely under way. Frustration turned to anger, building up a head of steam inside him. He was psyched up, ready to explode. If he was going to do something, there would never be a better time than—

He rushed the big man, holding his knife out of range

from a kick, watching hands and feet all at once. The enemy stood waiting for him, foolishly, making a stationary target when he should have been retreating, ducking off to one side or the other, *something*. If he just stood there—

He didn't.

As the stalker lunged, the big man gripped his wrist some-how, a blur of motion from his left hand, and the world turned upside down. A wobbly somersault ended with blunt-force impact on the ground, driving the air from his lungs again.

Before the stalker had a chance to catch his breath, a knee was on his chest, the curved blade pressed against his throat.

"One chance," the winner told him. "What's your name?"

It came out as a whisper.

"Jason Claridge."

BOLAN SCANNED THE FACE beneath the war paint, seeking points in common with the photographs he'd studied. Maybe something in the eyes, a trace around the mouth. Without the name, he would've missed it.

"You're the son?" he asked.

A breathless rasp came back at him.

Bolan rose and stepped back from the supine form, but kept the bolo in his hand. No question to it, he said, "You're looking for your parents."

"What do you—? Oh, God."

Whatever fight was left in Jason Claridge seemed to van-ish then. He lay still for a moment, eyes closed, trying to di-gest the circumstances. When he finally sat up, then clambered to his feet, there was a mix of anger and confu-sion on his painted face.

"They told me no one would be going in," he said. "It's standard policy."

"Subject to change without a press release," Bolan replied.

"Where are the others?" Claridge asked.

"I'm it."

"One man? Oh, Lord."

Bolan changed the subject. "What are you?"

"You called it. I'm the son. Their one and only."

"I was thinking of your unit."

"Navy SEALs," Claridge replied. "And yours?"

"I'm off the books."

"A spook?"

"How long have you been AWOL?"

"Four days. They told me no one would be going in. I had to try."

"What's your extraction plan?" Bolan asked.

"I don't have one," Claridge said. "I'm on my own here, as you may have noticed."

"Right. So, you just planned to walk around the island until you found your folks, then save them from the heavies by yourself and swim back to the States."

"Somebody had to make an effort."

"Someone has."

"I didn't *know* that."

"You've been trained for special ops," Bolan replied. "Whoever said you'd always be informed?"

"I could've helped."

"Meaning you could've butted in and made a nuisance of yourself. Like now."

"It's family, all right? Maybe you don't know how that feels."

Bolan was long past being baited on the subject of his kin, even by those who knew the score. "You need to get out while you can," he said.

"There's no extraction plan, remember?"

"Head for the Malaysian border, north across the mountains." Bolan pointed vaguely. "Ditch the gear and scrub the war paint off before you get there. Tell them you're a botanist who lost his way and ask for someone from the U.S. Embassy."

"I'd rather stay and help," Claridge replied.

"It's not an option."

"Think about it. You say one man hasn't got a chance, but here you are, going against an army on your own."

"It's different. I've done this sort of thing before."

"Still couldn't hurt to have somebody watch your back."

"No, thanks. Go home."

Claridge stiffened, gaining another inch. His shoulders squared. "I'm not leaving."

"Maybe the SEALs are glad to have you AWOL, if you always act like this."

"Like what?"

"The words that come to mind are unprofessional and insubordinate."

"Stow that. I don't see any rank insignia."

"Would it make any difference?"

Claridge considered it, and then said, "No."

"You've made my point."

"Listen, I watch the news, okay? I know how these things go. I won't run out and leave my parents here to die. They're all I have!"

"You don't know where to look."

"But you do, right?" The tone was hopeful now.

"Hear this. My job is to extract your parents, not to babysit. You haven't shown me anything so far, except an attitude that's put you on the fast track to a court-martial. Right now, I can't trust you to crack an MRE, much less to watch my back or follow orders in the crunch."

"Try me."

"I've got no use for wild cards."

"Hey, you call the game. I'm in your hands."

The Executioner digested it. He realized the son was never going to walk away. He relented just enough to say, "If you sign on for this, we need an understanding, you and I. From now until we're on the freedom bird, my word is law. The *only* law. If I say jump, you don't take time to ask, 'How high?'"

"No sweat."

"Hear me and understand," Bolan said, pressing on. "My one and only mission is to get your parents out. As far as I'm concerned, they never had a son. You're just another grunt. First time you slow me down or drop a stitch, I'll fix it so the problem doesn't happen twice."

"Agreed. If I screw up, I'm on my own."

"You still aren't listening," Bolan corrected him. "If you screw up, you're dead."

"Sounds fair," the son replied.

"Fair doesn't enter into it. Out here, you live or die. There's no third option."

"Understood."

"I hope so. Grab your piece, and let's get moving."

"Where are we going?"

"South," Bolan said. "To the end of the line."

SERGEANT MOHAMMED SINGH called his squad to a halt. A fine rain had started. There was mist on his face, drifting down from the canopy far overhead. He feared it would worsen before much time passed, adding insult to injury.

They had been tricked. That much was obvious. Someone had baited them, and Singh had fallen for the trick as if he were a green recruit.

"What is it, Sergeant-sir?" one of the privates asked.

"Nothing," he said. "There's nothing, Private."

"But we heard it, sir."

Singh offered no response. He knew they'd heard the noise, of course. His order had sent them racing after it like children through the forest, all to no avail. He tried to think it through, weigh odds and angles, to decide what he should do.

"Sergeant?"

"Be quiet! Let me think!"

"Yes, sir."

There was a possibility that he had been mistaken, Singh decided. Perhaps, though he considered it unlikely, the sounds they had pursued were made by some wild animal.

Something with four legs and a tail.

In that case, he'd been careless, maybe even foolish, but there would be no harm done in the long term.

If it had been a man who made the sounds, though, that would be a very different matter. In that case, he'd been outwitted by a clever fellow, possibly an enemy who still remained at large. Ignoring such a person, when he'd been dispatched specifically to find unwelcome visitors, could rebound to his detriment.

"Gather around," he told the troops, and waited while they formed a ring around him in the drizzling rain. Their faces, weary but expectant, told Singh they would follow any order he gave.

"We have a choice to make," he said. "I have the authority to make it for you, but I seek your guidance, since the outcome of the choice affects you all."

They waited, puzzled. Singh had never given them a choice before. It was unprecedented, verging on incomprehensible.

"What is it, Sergeant-sir?" the corporal asked.

The moment was unique in Singh's experience. He hoped it would remain so. "It is possible," he said, "that we have pursued an animal by accident, and now it's given us the slip. If so, there is no more for us to do but return to base camp and be done with this search."

He saw the others sharing glances, clearly dubious, although they loved the jungle no more than he did. The thought of going back was welcome, but if they were going back to lie, it had a very different connotation. Clearly, most of them believed they had pursued a man or men on their dash through the forest.

"The other possibility," Singh continued, "is that we heard a man, perhaps the very man we were dispatched to find, and now we've lost him. In that case, we dare not stop until we find him or exhaust all means of searching for him, day and night. We must retrace our steps, find where he slipped away and make it right."

"But, Sergeant-sir," the corporal offered, hand raised like a child in a classroom, "shouldn't the choice be yours?"

"It is, of course. But since the choice has consequences, we must show a solid front. No muttering among you that we did too much or did not do enough. This time, if there are repercussions, we will all be under scrutiny."

He'd laid it on thick, deliberately so. Whatever scrutiny there was would fall on Singh alone, he realized, but this way he could share the weight, at least for now. It made him feel crafty and sly.

"What if it was a man, sir?" asked a private to his left.

Singh shrugged. "He may be just another villager. The 'falling man' may have been nothing. You know birders, how they are." Soft laughter from his men at that. "Or, then again, it may have been a rebel, maybe two. No more than that, I'm confident, or we'd have seen them, surely."

"Rebels always pass this way, sir," said the corporal.

"You're correct. And we catch some of them, while others get away. It's nothing new. Of course, the present situation makes it different."

Singh didn't have to tell them what he meant by that. Even the slowest private knew about the recent kidnapping of two Americans and had some vague idea of how it was affecting international relations. They'd been on alert since the event occurred, for all the good it did.

"And so," he asked, "what shall it be?"

The corporal was first to speak. "I think we heard a tapir, Sergeant-sir."

"A tapir, yes," one of the privates nearest to him echoed. Soon the rest were nodding and repeating it.

"A tapir?" Singh considered it, frowning. "I think you may be right, in which case there is nothing left for us to do. Corporal, tell base camp that we're coming home. The birder was mistaken."

DEFEAT WAS A BITTER PILL to swallow. Jason Claridge had been top of his class in SEAL training, gung-ho and ready for anything the Navy threw at him. He'd lived off the land, eaten rats and worms without complaint, and bested anyone who came at him in terms of physical strength. A certain arrogance was encouraged in that training, as long as it stopped short of independent thinking, and Claridge had come to think of himself as well-nigh invincible.

The past week had changed that, with a vengeance. First had come the news of his parents' kidnapping, followed closely by reaffirmation of the government line that negotiation with terrorists was forbidden. Rather than leave it to the bumbling locals, who'd been trying to suppress a native uprising since he was in diapers, Claridge had gone AWOL, flushed his career down the toilet, and made a beeline for the place where his parents were caged.

More or less.

Without official guidance, he was flying blind. Acquiring gear had been no problem. Slipping into Kalimantan from the north was easy, too, but after that the leads had petered out. One "source" had scammed him out of fifteen hundred dollars he would never see again, and that left him drifting, dreadfully aware of passing time, frightened more than anything that he would find his family one day too late.

Tracking the stranger was a whim, something to do when he had nothing else on tap. And it had paid off for him, serendipitously, although not as Claridge had expected. He'd been thinking he could trail the guy for a while, see where he went, and maybe get a lead on any rebels lurking in the neighborhood.

Instead, he'd got his ass kicked and might've had his throat slit, if the guy had been a straight-up enemy. It was the sort of thing that pissed off macho warriors and encouraged them to think in terms of payback, but he couldn't run with that.

Not here. Not now.

The stranger said his name was Matt Cooper. Claridge didn't know if that was true. What difference did it make? The only thing that mattered was Cooper's claim to know where they could find his parents. If that claim turned out to be a lie, there would be hell to pay.

But in the meantime, Claridge needed him.

Follow the leader hadn't been his favorite childhood game, but he had learned to live with it in basic training and the SEAL courses that followed. Military discipline was iron clad. Breaching it in combat meant that people died. Ordinarily he had no problem taking orders from a stranger, but three things rankled him about this situation.

First up, he didn't know if he could trust Cooper.

Second, if they failed, it would be his parents who suffered, not some faceless strangers.

And third, the guy had kicked his ass.

It hadn't been easy for him, exactly, but Claridge knew he should've taken out Cooper, even with the other's slim advantage of surprise. The guy was twice his age, but he had moves, believe it. And "strong" fell way short of describing his grip.

More than anything, though, Claridge had surrendered to those eyes. In sparring matches, he could always tell how serious an adversary was by checking out the eyes. Most held a measure of amusement, tempered with determination. Now and then, a crazy one turned on the Manson lamps and Claridge had to put him down without a lot of fancy footwork, finish it before someone got hurt. The eyes had it.

And Matt Cooper's eyes were cold.

Staring into those depths with a razor-edged blade at his throat, Claridge had known that Cooper would kill him unless he caved in. He hadn't guessed it. All he had to do was look, and there it was. His death. And he had known that it would mean no more than stepping on a bug.

Nobody messed with eyes like that, if they had any sense at all. Not unless there was no other choice, and they'd done all they could to stack the odds in their favor.

But for now, it was a waiting game. Trailing a stranger through the jungle, looking for the scattered pieces of his life.

And it was raining. Hard.

It wasn't hot, the way most people pictured jungle rain. He had been sweating like a pig before the cloudburst started, but the rain had shaved an easy ten degrees off of the temperature, maybe fifteen. After the sun went down, if it kept raining, he could forget heatstroke and start to worry about hypothermia.

Lord, give me strength.

That was something his father would've said, and the apple fell close to the tree. A casual observer wouldn't know it, watching him in action with a squad of fellow SEALs, but Jason Claridge had his parents' faith. He trusted God to help him do whatever the Almighty wanted done.

But that was the rub.

Because nobody ever really knew what He was thinking when He pulled one of these stunts.

Until he *did* know, Jason Claridge was prepared to play a watching, waiting game and seize the opportunities that were presented to him.

But once he knew the rules, watch out.

"We can't go any farther in the dark," Bolan announced. "We'll camp here for the night. No fire."

He saw that Claridge didn't like it, and in fact he could've kept on marching through the night, despite the rain, but Bolan didn't want to risk it with a stranger on his heels. He'd made fair progress for his first day on the ground, and he hadn't been expecting enemy contact his first night in-country.

He was still on schedule, more or less, whether Claridge knew it or not.

"If you want to give me some coordinates," the young man said, "I don't mind scouting on ahead. Night work's no sweat."

"Forget it."

"Just like that?"

"That's it."

"You need to understand, this is my family."

"And you won't do them any good by blundering around until you're caught or killed. Do you think that would make them feel better, or worse?"

"I may surprise you."

"You already did," Bolan replied. "Once is enough."

"What stops me going on alone?"

"Good sense, if you've got any. Otherwise, the jungle."

Claridge said no more as Bolan found a relatively dry spot, underneath an ancient tree, and dug into his rucksack for an MRE. It wasn't gourmet food, by any stretch of the imagination, but it was designed to keep him going in the rough.

And it didn't get much rougher than this.

Claridge had rations of his own, something that crackled when he opened it and smelled a bit like sour fruit. When he was halfway through it, the young man reckoned it was time to talk again.

"I'd like to know who sent you, if it's not too much."

"What difference does it make?" Bolan asked.

"Maybe none. But if the government's dead set against involvement, why would they send someone out at all?"

"I never said they sent me."

"What am I supposed to think? You're not here on vacation, and I've got no other relatives who could've hired a merc to do the job. *Somebody* sent you."

"All that matters is, I'm here," Bolan replied. "I wasn't counting on a sidekick dropping in."

"Two pairs of hands, instead of one. How could it hurt?"

"Unless I have control over both pairs, the second could be worse than useless. It could ruin everything."

"I thought we'd settled that."

"I have your word," said Bolan. "Only time will tell me what it's worth."

"Point taken," Claridge said. "But think of this—I won't do anything to cause my parents harm."

"Not consciously, but you're involved, and that's a problem. There's a reason surgeons aren't allowed to operate on relatives."

"I won't go crazy. You can take that to the bank."

"No banks around here," Bolan said. "Just you and me."

"Still, you can trust me."

Bolan didn't answer.

He could've used the satellite uplink to contact Stony Man and check on Claridge, maybe even force the issue of a pickup to get the son out of his hair, but it would've further complicated an already complex situation. If he tried to press the issue, there was better than a fifty-fifty chance Claridge would slip away from him, and chasing a Navy SEAL through the Borneo jungle bore no resemblance to the mission he'd accepted from Brognola.

The young man might be strong and wise enough to keep

a lid on his emotions when he saw his parents or the camp where they were held. Bolan hoped so, but he would also be prepared to cope with any outbursts that occurred, before they snowballed into a full-blown disaster. If it came to choices, Bolan knew why he was here, and he would not be making any last-minute substitutions on the menu.

One way to look at it, he thought, was that Claridge gave him an out if the game went to Hell. He couldn't be responsible for eleventh-hour drop-ins who messed up the play—except, perhaps, in his own mind and heart.

Some soldiers liked to say that failure wasn't an option, but Bolan knew better. That kind of tough talk sounded good on television sound bites. It helped politicians get votes.

But it simply wasn't true.

Failure was always an option. Everybody failed sometime, at something. Pitchers might throw perfect games from time to time, but none had ever done it every time. None ever would.

Because humans were fallible, right down the line.

Failure was built into the mechanism, as certain as death.

And that, Bolan thought, was the ultimate failure.

He didn't plan to die in Borneo, but neither did he plan to live forever. Flesh and blood broke down, in time, the same as any other overworked machine. A lucky warrior went out at the top of his game, guns blazing, instead of lying in a bed somewhere, eaten from the inside out by some wasting disease.

It was a perk of putting on the uniform, whichever side he served: the chance to make an ordinary life—and death—count for something beyond the norm.

Bolan didn't know if Jason Claridge was prepared to make that kind of sacrifice on his parents' behalf. He talked the talk, but that was only part of it.

They would soon find out if he also walked the walk.

6

Garuda Malajit was furious. On average, he worked himself into a towering rage once a week, but the attacks had grown more frequent and more ferocious since he had ordered the arrest of the two American intruders. Rightfully, his temper should have been improved, but something had gone wrong.

It wasn't working out.

The first problem had been miscalculation on his part, which made his foul mood even worse. Malajit had believed that U.S. missionaries were dispatched around the world by wealthy churches tied to capitalist enterprise, paving the way for corporate invasions of the nonwhite world by making peasants pliable, content to labor through their days on Earth for subsistence wages, while they focused on the ultimate rewards of Heaven. Now, too late, he learned that some—at least the two he had selected for his exercise—went preaching on their own, or with the minimal support of congregations that could barely make ends meet.

It was bizarre, but he could not refute the facts. A contact in Jakarta had discovered that the Holy Ghost Revival possessed only 357, most of them on old-age pensions and the rest employed primarily at unskilled trades. They were the sort of people who would weep over a fallen minister, but who could not afford to ransom him.

That news had tipped Garuda Malajit into a fit of rage

that prompted him to shoot one of the dogs that hung around the camp, sniffing for scraps. But there was worse to come.

He understood the rhetoric of diplomats who claimed their governments did not negotiate with so-called terrorists. Malajit believed it was a pose adopted for the cameras. From personal experience, he knew that politicians lived on compromise and shady bargains. They would happily negotiate with anyone, as long as they could save face in the bargain and appear to strike a beneficial deal. Perhaps some aide to the U.S. ambassador would christen him a rebel or a freedom fighter, rather than a terrorist, and they could settle down to working out the ransom payment.

But it didn't happen.

Malajit's initial overture had been rebuffed in no uncertain terms, and the response from Washington had been emphatic. No negotiation, period. A spokesman for the U.S. President had gone on television with a demand for the immediate release of any hostages, further suggesting that the Sword of Freedom should disarm, disband and scatter to the winds.

It was too much.

That foolish ultimatum sent him storming from one end of camp to the other, raging at those who were slow to get out of his way. By the time he faced the prisoners, Malajit was livid, combustible and ready to explode.

As always, the American couple regarded him with curious expressions, mingling pity and resolve. He hated them and wished that he could shatter their complacency to see the fear inside.

"Your State Department tells me they don't care if you survive or not," he said, by way of introduction.

"You'll forgive me, brother, if I don't accept that," said the slender, gray-haired man.

"They will not pay for your release."

"I told you that, four days ago," the minister reminded him. "It's policy. They have a set of rules to follow, brother."

"I am *not* your brother!"

"We're all brothers in the eyes of Jesus."

"Yet your *brother* in the White House is prepared to sacrifice your lives. He values money over flesh and blood."

"I do believe he cares about us, but if he knuckles under for the likes of us, it just encourages people like you to take more hostages, commit more crimes."

Malajit's pulse was like a base drum, thumping in his ears. "You think fighting for freedom is a crime?" he asked.

"I don't know anything about your grievances," the preacher said. "But, brother—"

Only one short step, and Malajit was close enough to kick the American in the face. The impact stung his ankle, even with the high-top boots laced tightly, but it didn't matter. Malajit was glad to see the old man topple over backward, crimson jetting from his nose.

He drew back his leg to land another kick, but the woman lunged in front of him, the first time she had moved since Malajit entered their hut. She lunged across her husband's body, shielding him.

No matter.

Malajit was just as capable of kicking women, when the fury gripped him like a fist and squeezed the pulsing blood into his skull. Without missing a beat, he drove his boot into her ribs.

The old man struggled to help her, and Malajit lashed out with his right fist into the bloodied face, shouting as he hammered it.

"I'm not your brother! Say it! Tell your Jesus I am not his child and not your brother!"

Sometimes, when his soldiers found cause to restrain him, Malajit resisted them with every ounce of strength he had.

Today, however, when he felt their hands upon him, it was almost a relief. He let them turn him, lead him from the hut, and he saw Shaitan Takeri waiting for him just outside.

"See to them," Malajit instructed, then shook off his escorts and moved swiftly toward his quarters. He felt better, now that the storm had passed.

He wasn't finished yet.

If the White House would not negotiate, then he would simply have to find a way to change their minds.

THE RAIN STOPPED around midnight, and Bolan was ready to break camp before the first dim rays of dawn found their way through the thick jungle canopy. Claridge had spent a restless night, but he shook it off and shouldered his equipment with a grim determination Bolan recognized from other battlegrounds, throughout his War Everlasting.

The kid might make it, but he still bore watching.

Bolan wasn't letting down his guard.

He never did.

As they set out, Bolan ignored Claridge's questions about their destination. He didn't trust the SEAL's self-control far enough to entrust Claridge with the coordinates. It could be a recipe for disaster, perhaps forcing him to choose between the parents and the son in a moment when there was no time for lengthy debate or soul-searching.

Bolan wasn't sure that he could force himself to kill the young man, if it came down to a choice of either-or, but he could definitely wound Claridge, if the anxious son was about to blow his mission on an impulse.

The one thing he certainly didn't have time for was chasing an oversize child through the jungle, pleading with him to act like a grown-up and let the adults help his parents. SEAL-qualified or not, the moment Claridge let emotions override his training and his combat sense, he would become a liability.

And Bolan dealt with liabilities in no uncertain terms.

If he'd been in Jason Claridge's position, Bolan would doubtless have pursued the matter privately, as well, but that didn't mean that he trusted the young SEAL's judgment. His reading of Hal Brognola's brief file on the Claridge family told him that Jason had never been bloodied in combat, had never seen action of any kind on hostile ground, against real flesh-and-blood enemies. He was a well-trained, well-intentioned cherry, with a sentimental monkey riding on his back.

And that's what made him dangerous to both sides in this game of life and death.

Bolan saw the snake around the same time it saw him. He didn't recognize the species, but its thick triangular head told him it was a viper. Four feet, give or take an inch. Its color was the same gray-brown as the bark on the perch it was twined around, a face-high limb that jutted into Bolan's path.

He stopped and turned to Claridge. "We've got a snake," he said, and shifted to his left, circling the tree.

"Why don't you kill it?" Claridge asked him.

"There's no need."

"It's just a snake."

"Unless you plan to bring it with you, let it be."

Claridge blinked once, and then said, "Right. Trace evidence. I get it."

No, you don't. Bolan let it go.

The trail was what he made of it, using the wrist compass to keep him headed south-southwest, forging ahead wherever possible along the path of least resistance. Bolan could have used the bolo knife to hack his way and clear the trail for Claridge, but the marks he left behind would also blaze a trail for anyone who followed them.

And who would that be?

Bolan couldn't say, but there were definitely armed patrols out in the neighborhood. Whether they represented rebels,

government manhunters, or some other faction he was unaware of, Bolan didn't want to make things easy for them. If
they found him, they would have to work for it. And there
would be a battle waiting for them at trail's end.

He wondered whether Jason Claridge could pull his own
weight in the crunch, if he had what it took to kill and kill
again without tipping into the void and losing himself in the
process. SEALs were trained killers, but training and killing
were two different things. It was never the same with a
dummy, a firing range target, or a sparring partner swaddled
in padding.

When it came down to killing, a man either could, or he
couldn't. Most could, with the right motivation, but some
only needed the word. Some made it an art form, while others got off on the power.

Which kind was Jason Claridge?

There was only one way to find out, and Bolan hoped he
would be able to postpone that test as long as possible. If they
could pull off the mission without a fight, somehow, so much
the better.

But if they couldn't, Claridge would be forced to look out
for himself. The Executioner already had one job to do, and
it was plenty. If the young man couldn't cut it, he would fall
along the way.

And would his parents care at all for freedom, if they lost
their only son?

Tough choices.

They were part of Bolan's daily life. He took them as they
came, resolved them, and moved on. Like slipping through
the jungle, right, leaving as few traces as possible.

Like Death.

"AMOS? ARE YOU OKAY?"

He seemed to hear the voice from far away, as if it were

an echo in his mind from childhood. Mother lifting him when he had fallen from his bicycle and skinned his elbows raw.

"Amos?"

It hurt worse than his elbows, this time. Amos Claridge thought he had to have fallen harder than he could remember, landing on his head. That would explain the fierce, dull ache that churned behind his eyes—but what about his ribs?

"Amos!"

He opened his eyes, let them swim into focus on the face that hovered inches from his own.

"Merilee?"

"Oh, Amos. Thank God, you're alive!"

"What's happened, Merilee?"

She frowned at that, blinking through tears. He saw a dark bruise forming on the frail line of her jaw. "You don't remember, then?"

"I'm trying."

It came back to him in tatters then, but swiftly. In another moment, Amos Claridge had it all. He felt a rush of anger vying with the pain.

"That animal hurt you, as well?"

He bolted upright in her arms, then nearly fainted from the stab of agony between his ribs. It brought tears to his eyes unbidden. When he raised a shaky hand to swipe at them, Claridge felt fresh blood on his face.

"How bad is it?" he asked.

Her nurse's training kicked in automatically. "The bleeding from your nose has nearly stopped, but I'm afraid it's broken. You'd be a better judge about your ribs."

"They hurt a bit," he told her, working on a smile.

"They should." Her eyes were overflowing now. "You know I don't have any bandages."

"It doesn't matter, Merilee."

"I can't do anything to help you." Almost sobbing.

"You already have," he said. "How badly are you hurt?"

She smiled through her tears. "I'm tougher than I look."

"God knows that's true." The anger had receded to a dull ache in his chest. "Did he say anything about…what happens next?"

"Nothing. He's angry that the government won't pay, of course."

"I told them that. Liars don't recognize the truth. It goes against their nature."

"Amos—"

"Don't you worry, Merilee," he interrupted her. "Whatever happens, we're prepared to meet it in the armor of our faith."

Right now, that armor didn't feel too sturdy, but the very thought brought pangs of guilt to vie with physical discomfort. Doubting God in times of trial was a snare set for the righteous by their mortal enemy, old Satan. Amos Claridge had faced that temptation before, and he knew how to beat it.

"We must pray," he said. "Now, more than ever, we need Jesus."

"What if He's forsaken us?"

It startled him to hear the words spoken aloud. "You mustn't say that, Merilee. We mustn't even think it!"

"I suppose you're right."

"Pray with me now."

"Dear Lord…"

He faltered. For the first time in his life, Claridge could not think what to say. He knew the words, of course, but stringing them together was a challenge that defeated him.

Suppose God *had* abandoned them. Suppose their faith was insufficient to warrant deliverance from this trial. What would he do in that case? Was there anything his poor flesh could accomplish in the present situation?

"Amos?"

"I…I don't…" He gave up, shook his head and closed his eyes against the burning, bitter tears.

Praying for strength to die wasn't the kind of thing they taught in Bible school. It shamed him that he couldn't speak the words.

The Lord helps those who help themselves.

But what could he do in the present situation, beyond praying and waiting to see what happened next? Amos knew he didn't have the power or the courage to vanquish his enemies, not even for Merilee's sake. They were too many, too strong, and too well armed.

It was the sense of helplessness that made him feel unworthy, worse than any pain his captors could inflict.

There was only one good thing about their present situation, Amos decided. At least their son couldn't see them like this.

"So, YOU FOUND NOTHING, then? Nothing at all?"

Major Rajak Tripada waited, watching the subject closely. Sergeant Mohammed Singh was a defender of the state, but Tripada had worked internal security long enough to know that no one was above suspicion. Everyone had weaknesses that might betray them in a crisis.

"Nothing, sir," the sergeant replied. "As I've said, we heard sounds in the forest and followed, but no one was there. I think it was a tapir, or perhaps a tiger."

"There are no tigers on Borneo, Sergeant."

"One hears stories, sir. The birders—"

"Ah, yes," Tripada interrupted him. "The birders. It was one of them who saw this falling man, I understand."

"One thought he saw a man, sir. Some of them imagine things. They're foreigners, most of them, sir, and unfamiliar with the wildlife of the islands."

"Still, it's difficult, confusing men and birds, wouldn't you say, Sergeant?"

"Perhaps, sir. I can't say."

"This noise you heard. Can you describe it for me?"

"Thrashing in the undergrowth, sir. Something running, I suppose."

"You never caught a glimpse, though?"

"No, sir."

"How unfortunate. You know about the missionaries who were kidnapped, don't you, Sergeant?"

"Yes, sir. We were briefed the day it happened."

"You're familiar with the Sword of Freedom, I suppose?"

"I wouldn't say familiar, sir. I know they're traitors to the state. I've never met one of them, to my knowledge. We go looking for them in the mountains, but we haven't caught them yet."

"And why is that, do you suppose?" Tripada asked.

"I reckoned we had poor intelligence to work with, sir."

"You don't think much of our security police, then?"

He saw the trap. Singh shrugged and said, "I don't think much about it one way or another, sir. I lead patrols where I am told to go. If we find nothing, I suppose that someone was mistaken. It is not my place to question orders. Someday, when the enemy is located, I'll meet him on the battlefield."

"That day may be upon you sooner than you think, Sergeant."

"I'm ready, sir!"

"When did you know that you had lost this shadow in the jungle?"

"When the noise stopped, sir. We searched about and could find nothing to suggest a man had passed that way, so we gave up."

"I see." Tripada pinned the sergeant's eyes with his and held them for another moment, then flashed a disarming smile and said, "That's all. You are dismissed."

"Yes, sir!"

They exchanged formal salutes and the sergeant departed,

closing the door behind him. Alone once more, Tripada thought about what he had learned—or, more precisely, what he had not learned from the debriefing.

He did not believe the sergeant was a traitor, but he knew the man was holding something back. Best guess, he had grown tired of trekking through the jungle and decided that the mission was a waste of time. Whether the noise he had pursued was animal or human, it was now impossible to say. To that extent, at least, the exercise had been a waste.

That didn't mean, however, that the search should be called off.

Major Tripada understood his enemies. The men who joined the Sword of Freedom were impatient, sometimes even reckless. They craved recognition and acknowledgment. They made demands and then threw bloody tantrums when they didn't get their way. To that extent, they were like children armed with adult weapons, lethal and pathetic, all at once. Tripada did not sympathize, but he could play the parent's role and discipline them sternly.

He would crush them, if he got the chance.

The recent kidnapping was both an obstacle and opportunity, in his opinion. While the politicians fretted over whether it would cost them U.S. aid, Tripada saw it as a motivator for the all-out war against guerrillas that he'd advocated in advance of the event. So far, his colonel had demurred, fearing how watchdogs from the human rights groups might react to an offensive. Now, with pressure on from Washington, all things were possible.

It was a time for wiping slates and settling old scores. But he would have to find his targets first, before the killing could begin.

Upon his signal, the next man through the door was Mahmoud Kendik. He was a ferret of a man, all smirks and oily charm beneath a strangler's eyes. Kendik was an informer, a

turncoat for hire. Most recently, he'd been a member of the
Sword of Freedom, claiming knowledge of the outfit's lead-
ership and movements.

"Major, I've been waiting for your call," he said, smiling.

"Sit down," Tripada ordered, pleased to see the smile slip
out of place. "I wish to take advantage of your knowledge and
your offer to assist the government."

"A pleasure, sir."

"It may be," said Tripada. "But I promise you, Mahmoud,
that if you cause me any measure of embarrassment, the pleasure will be brief. And what comes after it will make your
worst nightmares seem tame."

"I understand, of course, sir."

"Good. You won't receive another warning. Now, as if
your life depended on the answer, tell me where to find these
so-called friends of yours."

JASON CLARIDGE WAS fighting fatigue as they broke camp
that morning and got on the move once again. He'd dozed off
several times during the night, but hadn't really slept. Between the rain and jungle noises, his suspicions of Matt
Cooper, and the fears that haunted him about his parents'
safety, there'd been no real hope for rest.

It had been like that, more or less, since he'd received the
news. The first night, when he still thought there was hope of
a solution through government channels, he'd lain awake and
tried to picture what they had to be suffering. He knew nothing about Indonesian politics or social turmoil, and next to
nothing about the terrain, except that it had some things in
common with the rest of Southeast Asia. His general knowledge of terrorists was likewise restricted by the Navy's need-
to-know instruction format.

The bottom line: commandos weren't expected to analyze
their targets, or even think of them as human beings. They

were objects to be neutralized, and as such, their political opinions were irrelevant. If Uncle Sam pointed a finger and demanded that an Arab, a Chinese or Nicaraguan should be taken out with all dispatch, the SEAL team sent to do the job wasn't expected to debate the wisdom of the hit or judge the target for themselves.

Get in. Get done. Get out.

Those were the simple rules of special ops, and Jason Claridge had no problem with them when he joined the SEAL program. The Good Book was filled with mighty warriors who had also served their Lord, from Joshua to David and beyond. Despite coarse language in the barracks, the delight some of his comrades took in alcohol and fornication, Claridge still believed that it was possible to serve both God and country, in the proper circumstances.

But he'd thrown all that away for his parents' sake. If he gave up and went back to his unit on the first flight out of Borneo, the very best he could expect was brig time on the AWOL charges and expulsion from the SEAL program. They probably wouldn't discharge him, all things considered, but he'd spend the rest of his blighted career swabbing decks or filing nonsensitive papers in some captain's office.

He'd never be trusted again, that was certain.

Not with anything that mattered.

And since he'd blown it anyway, he might as well press on and see the mission through to its conclusion.

What would that be? Claridge didn't have a clue. He didn't know where they were going, if his parents waited for them at their journey's end, or if so, how many hostiles would be guarding them. This was another part of the rescue he hadn't thought through when the first impulse to help had seized him. In fact, beyond the mechanics of going AWOL and making his way to Borneo, he'd done no real planning at all.

Could two men pull off the rescue?

He supposed they'd have a better chance than one alone, but he had to admit that the jungle made him feel tiny, childlike. He knew the raw stats on the island—population, climate, area, the kind of things available on any of a dozen Web sites—but none of it prepared him for the stark reality of living in the bush.

The jungle dwarfed him, swallowed him alive, and Claridge wondered whether it would ever let him go. Would he be living when it spit or shat him out? Could he do anything to help his parents, or had he come all this way to sacrifice the final member of his bloodline?

One thing was certain in his mind: He had to try.

If there'd been any other choice, the prospect of effective intervention, there was no way he'd have broken ranks to tackle such a quest alone.

That made him think about Matt Cooper, thirty yards ahead of him and moving through the forest as if he'd been born there. What made him so confident that he could do a better job alone than with a combat-trained companion?

Experience, for one thing, Claridge thought.

The cold eyes and that grip of steel spoke volumes. Claridge didn't think they would be sharing war stories around the campfire, and he had none to contribute if they did, but he still recognized the real deal when he saw it.

He'd met a few such men in training and on posts where he had served. Men who'd plied their trade in Vietnam, Grenada, Desert Storm, Somalia, and a string of covert ops that went unnamed. They didn't wear special insignia, there was no "killer" badge or medal, but he'd come to recognize the look and attitude.

Cooper had been around, and he'd spilled blood. Claridge would bet his life on that.

In fact, he realized, that's what he had already done. Without intending it, he had become a part of Matt Cooper's campaign, his own mission co-opted in the process. It shouldn't matter, since they both sought to rescue his parents, but Cooper's motives were veiled, completely impersonal. And that made him a wild card to Claridge, as much as Claridge was to Cooper.

I've got my eye on you, thought Claridge. I'm not letting down my guard.

And so they passed on through the jungle's realm of shadows, two grim strangers bound by mutual suspicion and distrust.

7

Another damned patrol. There was no end to it, Shaitan Takeri thought.

At least none that he cared to contemplate.

The kidnapping had thus far gained them nothing but a pair of hostages they had to feed, however meagerly, and who incited their commander's deadly rage. It wouldn't be long now, Takeri guessed, before the generals in Jakarta made some concentrated move against the Sword of Freedom, to impress their paymasters in the United States.

And what would happen then?

More killing, which Takeri didn't mind, unless he wound up being one of those feeding ants and worms. Death came to everyone, of course, but he was young enough to hope that it would call on others first, before it came to him.

No matter how he looked for ways to make the situation better, nothing came to mind. They could release the prisoners and hope for mercy, but the Indonesian government had not been merciful to any adversary within living memory. The prisons and graveyards were filled with those who looked for justice in Takeri's homeland.

It would be simpler to eliminate the hostages, then pull up stakes and find another place to hide. Wait out the storm and then resume their struggle with the enemy. But would it make a difference to the outcome?

There was no answer, so Takeri focused on the forest trail in front of him. It was a track so narrow that it forced his men to walk in single file, ideal for an ambush. The good news was that government forces were rarely that clever. Instead of staking out a jungle path and waiting hours or days for their enemy to show they preferred raiding villages, shooting or arresting the peasants fingered as rebels by some faceless informer, torching their homes and leaving raw wounds behind when they left.

Garuda liked to say that the Indonesian army was his best recruiting tool, because they made lifelong enemies wherever they went. It was true, to a point, but most jungle-dwelling peasants still suffered in silence, buried their dead and went on with their hand-to-mouth lives. A few joined the Sword, others helped when they could with supplies, but most were like the two caged Americans: caught in the cross fire with nowhere to hide.

The patrols were defensive, Garuda always said, to prevent surprise attacks on their campsite. Takeri didn't question it, though he was wise enough to pierce the superficial logic. Any contact with their adversaries near the camp would simply help pinpoint the target, while the main thrust would inevitably come by air, with rockets and machine guns and troop carriers.

Still, he supposed it was better to do something, rather than sit around the camp and wait to hear the helicopters approach.

When that day came, Takeri meant to sell his life dearly. And he wouldn't mind killing a couple of Yankee intruders to kick off the game.

Unlike most of the men he'd chosen for his squad, Shaitan Takeri was a city boy. Born and raised in Banjarmasin, on the island's southern coast, he'd grown up in the city's teeming slum and met Garuda Malajit when they were two young thieves, uneducated, wandering the filthy streets by night and day. Takeri killed his first man in a mugging, at the tender age of fifteen years, and there had been no turning back.

He liked the revolution better, though. It gave him ample

opportunity to vent his rage, while cloaking anything he did in the guise of a struggle for freedom.

In his rare retrospective moments, Takeri supposed there was only one great difference between himself and the generals he hated with every fiber of his being. They had wealth and power, while he schemed to snatch it from their grasp.

What else were revolutions really all about?

The jungle did its best to smother him, but he had learned to live with the humidity, the mud that tried to pull his boots off every time he took a step, insects humming ceaselessly around his head. His brothers in the city had the same heat, same humidity. They lived with flies and roaches, human waste and bodies in the gutters.

They were victims, while Takeri had moved on and learned to fight.

Whether he had the strength to win was anybody's guess.

Meanwhile, he would patrol, and hope that there was no one waiting for him in the forest, watching over gunsights as he made his way along the narrow trail.

And if he made it back to camp alive, the next day he would play the game again.

BOLAN HEARD THE ENEMY coming and raised a clenched fist. Behind him, Claridge froze in place and waited, as silent as a stone.

Jungle fighting was divided into equal parts of art and science. The mechanics of it dealt with tools and weapons, transportation and communication, the logistics of a war fought on terrain and in a climate where every aspect of nature was potentially hostile. From Guadalcanal to the Congo and the Mekong Delta, conquering jungles had become a career in itself for certain military analysts and technicians.

But science could only take a warrior so far. On the ground, where it mattered, the grunts still had to know what they were doing, and that meant reading the jungle, making instant life-or-death decisions based on the snap of a twig or the flight of an insect. Was a sound hostile or neutral? Was that shadow cast by hanging vines, or by a lurking predator?

Bolan couldn't see the enemy yet, but he knew they were coming. As with the last patrol he'd dodged, the members of this team were careless in the little ways that got men killed. Some of them hadn't taped their gear to keep canteens or magazines from rattling slightly as they walked. They slashed at overhanging ferns from time to time, heedless. Birds and monkeys fled before them in a rush that might've passed for play with one less experienced.

Bolan scoped his surroundings for cover and didn't find much. They could step off the track anywhere and get lost in the jungle ten feet from the point where he stood, but real cover—the kind that stopped bullets and shrapnel—was pitifully sparse.

He had a choice to make, and Bolan made it. Turning to face Claridge, he used hand signals to dictate the play. Claridge followed it, nodded and moved to his right, easing into the backdrop of green. Bolan went to the left, taking pains not to make undue noise. Near-silence counted now, more than ever, with the hunters almost upon him.

Concealment was the only plan. He didn't go for distance, didn't seek an advantageous field of fire. If they could hide and let the hunters pass, he would be satisfied.

And if they couldn't, well, at least they were fairly well fixed for a cross fire.

He carried the Steyr AUG with a round in the chamber, easing off the safety and silently thumbing the fire-selector switch to 3-round bursts. It conserved ammunition and gave him more control in situations where the targets might be moving, half-hidden or worse, with a friendly somewhere on the far side of the firing line.

He hoped Claridge had sense enough to do the same.

Closer.

He waited, kneeling in the shadow of a tree that gave him partial cover, still nothing to write home about. This close, the hunting party sounded like a dozen men, at least. Those odds weren't insurmountable, by any means, but it was still a dicey situation, more so with a rookie on his hands.

It could be worse, if those approaching from the south were scouts, not hunters. That would mean a larger party coming up behind them, maybe large enough to sweep the area in force and root out trespassers. In that case, do-or-die might well come down to do-*and*-die.

Okay, then.

Bolan was prepared for anything that came his way.

He couldn't speak for Jason Claridge, though.

Footsteps immediately to his right made Bolan hold his breath. He didn't really think they'd hear him breathing, but it was a natural reflex. A moment later, when he silently exhaled, the first soldier in line was no more than five yards in front of him.

Another followed, and another. Bolan waited, counting heads, ready to fire from point-blank range if any of them glanced his way and showed the slightest sign of recognition. Each one of them had the potential to unmask him, but they seemed to focus on the trail exclusively, each keeping eyes locked on the man in front of him, as if afraid of getting lost.

If they were scouting, it was big-time negligence, but Bolan couldn't read their minds. For all he knew, this crew was heading home after a long day in the bush, thinking of nothing more than chow and clean, dry socks.

The passing glimpses of their uniforms and gear told Bolan they weren't regulars. They sported no insignia, and they were armed with AK-47s, while the Indonesian military got most of its hardware from the States.

Rebels.

He counted fifteen men and saw the last one pass by before it went to hell. Just when he thought they might be clear, a shout rose from the jungle to his left, immediately smothered by a short burst from a CAR-15.

Bolan pushed through the fragile shield of greenery and went to join the fight.

CLARIDGE WAS READY to congratulate himself for staying silent and immobile while the hostiles passed him, when the last guerrilla broke ranks, veering from the track and toward his hiding place.

Claridge held his fire, waiting another beat to find out what the trouble was. At this range, there was no way he could miss by accident.

The straggler stopped, slung his Kalashnikov over one shoulder and got busy with his fly. The zipper made a rasping sound, followed a second later by the spatter sounds of sweet relief.

Claridge waited, watching, afraid to move a muscle. He was almost close enough to touch the other man, but still partly concealed. The straggler had his eyes cast downward, taking care of business, but he wouldn't have to turn from where he stood to make eye contact. All he had to do was raise his head and glance off to his right, twenty degrees or so. If he did that—

A final shake, and Claridge heard the zipper closing. He was almost trembling with relief, when the guerrilla stretched, arms raised above his head…and met the watcher's eyes.

The shouted warning had a choked-off quality about it, gibberish as far as Claridge was concerned. He fired on reflex, caught the rebel reaching back for his rifle and put him down with four rounds to the chest.

Easy.

Except, it wasn't over yet.

He heard the others shouting, thrashing in the shrubbery. Fourteen gunners sprayed the trees and undergrowth with everything they had, the racket of their AKs blending into a cacophony of death.

Claridge went down, heard bullets ripping through the greenery a foot or two above his head. No targets visible, but he knew where the fire was coming from, spread out along a line some twenty yards in length and broadening as shooters scattered off the slender vestige of a trail.

Surrounding him.

A flash of panic that he'd never felt in training left him momentarily disoriented. Was he flanked already? Would his foes encircle him before he had a chance to break the ring and save himself? Where was Cooper in the midst of this? Had he been killed or wounded in the first barrage of fire?

Dear God, am I alone?

The months of practice kicked in, then, and none too soon. Claridge saw furtive movement in the shadows to his right and knew it was impossible that Cooper could've leapfrogged his position.

Hostiles, then.

He fired another short burst at the half-seen target, saw it lurch and fall as he was rolling to his right, seeking another vantage point. Several streams of auto-fire converged on his last-known position, chopping through leaves, vines and stalks.

The litany ran through his head. Stay mobile. Pick your targets. Short bursts. Make them count. All good advice, but keeping track of it when hostile shooters meant to blow his head off was another game entirely. Even when they used live fire in training, it had never been like this. No one had ever really tried to kill him during practice.

Jesus, give me strength!

A shadow lunged at Claridge from behind a nearby tree. He didn't know how one of them had gotten so close, undetected, and he had no time to think about it now. Instead of simply shooting him, the rebel tried to brain Claridge with his rifle. It was a dumb move, but it nearly worked, forcing Claridge to block the caveman swing and fall back, stumbling, to the ground.

The stranger was on top of him, swinging his piece again. What was he thinking? Was it jammed? Claridge absorbed the impact with his CAR-15 and hoped it wouldn't bend the magazine or knock the firing mechanism out of line. He slammed a boot into his adversary's hip or groin, he couldn't tell, but either way it hardly slowed the rebel.

Fingers were scrabbling at his weapon now, the AK-47 gone somehow. Instead of trying to disarm him, though, the guy on top of Claridge threw his weight atop the CAR-15 and tried to jam it underneath his chin. It wouldn't take much pressure there to crush his windpipe like a cardboard tube and leave him gasping out the final moments of his life.

A desperate heave unseated his opponent, Claridge groping for the knife he wore taped to his Alice rig. He found it, drew it from the leather sheath and buried it between his adversary's ribs.

SHAITAN TAKERI HAD NO idea where the first shots had come from, even less what his men were firing at now. Those he could see were shooting in all directions, muzzle-flashes blazing in the jungle gloom, while bullets flayed the undergrowth around them.

Takeri had been firing, too, until he realized he had no targets and was wasting precious ammunition he might need to save his life. Now he crouched behind the bole of a great tree and tried to make sense of the action around him.

The first shots, he knew, had not been fired by one of his

men. He knew the sound of a Kalashnikov by heart, and that burst had sounded more like a government weapon, one of the American-made M-16s. Still, if they were surrounded by troops, why weren't more of their enemies firing? Why were they even still alive?

Takeri heard one of the lighter rifles speak again and saw a member of his squad collapse, twitching in his death throes. He couldn't trace the fatal shots, had no way to respond except for wild firing into the jungle like his men, but Takeri resisted the impulse.

He needed a target. Someone he could see, and thus kill. Mad blasting at the trees was doubly dangerous, not only wasting ammunition but alerting hidden adversaries to his whereabouts.

Shaitan Takeri was no coward, but he wasn't suicidal, either. He intended to survive the revolution, if he could, and see what happened afterward. Sometimes that meant choosing his battles and deciding which objectives justified a certain risk.

Another of his men went down, and then another. While he couldn't see them all, Takeri knew the squad was being whittled down, and there was nothing to suggest they had inflicted matching damage on their enemies. So far, he didn't know how many shooters were involved in the ambush, where they were hidden, who they were.

He knew one thing: to save himself, Takeri had to make a choice and make it soon.

To join his men in battle, he had to hurry, while enough of them remained to make a stand or fight their way clear of the trap. To save himself, he had to leave soon, before the enemy ran out of targets and began to search the battleground.

Swiftly, Takeri weighed his options and the risks involved. If he returned to camp alone, he'd need a convincing story for Malajit and the rest, to explain his survival. A head wound, perhaps? He could claim he was stunned and awoke when the killing was finished. The enemy had overlooked him or left him for dead. Who could say, since he hadn't been conscious? If others escaped, they'd be hard pressed to challenge his story.

And if he stayed to fight...

It was no contest.

Choice made, Takeri wasted no time translating his plan into action. He crept away from the trail with all possible stealth, circling wide around the sounds of battle, offering a silent prayer to long-forgotten gods that he would not stumble across another ambush party in the forest.

What he needed now was speed.

There would be time enough to fake an injury along the way, before he reached the camp.

And Garuda Malajit would be happy to see him, would count himself lucky to have such a comrade. One who risked everything to warn his allies of impending danger.

He deserved a hero's welcome for his efforts.

But first, he had to get back alive.

THE CHATTER OF A CAR-15 told Bolan that the rebels hadn't finished Jason Claridge yet. He knew approximately where the young man was, but he could not have vouched for Jason's health or state of mind. Survival was the top priority right now, and that meant taking out the enemy before a radio alert or the percussive sounds of battle brought more heat down on his head.

In front of him, three enemies had gone to ground below eye level, in a washed-out gully on the east side of the trail. A fallen tree also protected them on Bolan's side. In fact, it was the kind of cover he'd been hoping for when he heard soldiers moving toward him through the jungle.

It was decent cover, but it wasn't perfect.

Nothing ever was.

Bolan palmed one of his frag grenades. They were the standard U.S.-manufactured M-67s, selected in equal measure for familiarity and because they were found in large numbers throughout Indonesia, purchased or stolen, employed by all sides. The choice preserved deniability if he was killed or captured, and if Bolan used them up, the evidence would self-destruct. A crime lab could've traced the shrapnel, but he knew damned well that no one would be picking fragments out of trees and analyzing them.

He pulled the pin, lined up his pitch and waited for a lull in firing from the ditch before he let it fly. Grenades were a mixed blessing in a jungle firefight. They scored hits that marksmanship might not have managed, sometimes, but the trees and undergrowth were also obstacles, deflecting careless throws and cushioning destructive force.

It wouldn't matter if he dropped the egg into their laps, though, and he gave it his best shot.

The pitch was decent, call it ninety-five out of a hundred points for accuracy and technique. The lethal egg fell short, but only by a foot or so, and impact with the massive log bounced it over the top. There was a fleeting hesitation, while the last two seconds on the fuse ran out, and then the charge went off.

It wasn't like the movies, bodies somersaulting through the smoky air, but real life almost never matches art. For one thing, Hollywood explosions were exaggerated to the point that a grenade containing six ounces of Compound B somehow attained the power of a ten-pound satchel charge. Likewise, those tumbling stunt men launched themselves from trampolines, while pyrotechnics went off in the background, unrelated to their flight.

So this was nothing like the movies, but it did the job. A sturdy thump of sound, some mud and mangled foliage pitched aloft, and then a wailing voice began to call for help. At least, that's what Bolan assumed the man was saying, since he didn't speak the language.

Close enough.

He went to help.

Crawling across the killing ground was risky, but his handful of surviving adversaries kept most of their aimless fire around chest height. He wondered how they'd lasted this long in a jungle war.

He reached the log and drew his pistol, weighted with the bulk of its suppressor. Just beyond his line of sight, the wails had tapered off to moans, but that was simply noise. It didn't mean his enemies were down and out. They weren't dead until Bolan either saw them dead or made them dead, with his own hands.

He paused again, then braced himself and rolled across the log, dropping into a crouch beyond it. There were three men in the gully, two of them already dead or on the verge of death from shrapnel wounds. The third, the moaner, had somehow escaped the main brunt of the blast, but he'd suffered a thigh wound and his crimson fingers weren't stopping the strong pulse of blood from the femoral artery.

Surprised, the rebel gaped at Bolan, but he didn't try to reach the AK-47 lying at his side. He was already slipping into shock, and Bolan calculated he'd be dead within five minutes, give or take.

Why wait?

The Glock coughed once and drilled a clean hole through the dying soldier's forehead. It may've been imagination, but the startled face seemed to reveal a vague expression of relief.

Bolan holstered the Glock and picked up his rifle, moving past the corpses to the gully's end that put him nearest to the trail. He was below the hostile line of fire there, but he still saw one—no, two—of his opponents crouching in the shadows, firing downrange toward someone or something beyond Bolan's view.

Claridge?

As he rose from the gully, one of the shooters glanced back and said something he couldn't understand. It didn't sound hostile, and Bolan assumed he'd been mistaken for one of the men he'd just killed. Instead of answering, he stitched the gunman with a 3-round burst and dropped him thrashing to the forest floor.

That got the other one's attention, but he wasn't fast enough to save himself. Bolan had target acquisition by the time the guy began to turn, fumbling with his Kalashnikov, and three more 5.56 mm rounds ended the contest in one second flat.

Getting there, he thought, but not done yet.

THE KNIFE BLADE MADE a little slurping sound as Jason Claridge pulled it free. Fighting the sudden rush of bile that stung his throat, he poised to strike again, but found it wasn't necessary. His last stoke had found some vital organ, he supposed. The man sprawled over him was dead.

He shoved away the leaking corpse and struggled to all fours. His camouflage fatigues were smeared with blood and something else he didn't want to think about. There was no time to dwell on it, in any case, for he could hear more soldiers closing in from either side.

Sheathing the bloody knife, Claridge scooped up his CAR-15 and fired into the jungle on his right, greeting the nearer of his adversaries with a spray of copper-jacketed projectiles. Someone squealed and then fell heavily, still screened from view by tattered undergrowth.

Behind him, dangerously close, an AK-47 blazed away at Claridge, spitting ten rounds per second through the shadows.

At that rate, it only took three seconds to exhaust a fully loaded magazine, and Claridge waited, facedown in the mud, until his enemy had to stop and reload.

It worked in theory, but he hadn't counted on another mindless rush. This time, though, Claridge heard the madman coming and was ready for him, lining up his shot before the young berserker burst upon him. Claridge fired the last rounds in his own mag at a range of fifteen feet and left his would-be slayer stretched out on the turf.

Reloading, he was suddenly aware that silence had descended on the battlefield. It was true silence, this time, since the forest animals and insects had been shocked by the explosive clash of human beings.

No, that wasn't right.

Someone was moving through the forest, coming closer. One man, by the sound of it, though Claridge didn't really trust his ringing ears.

He thought of changing his position, then decided that it wasn't worth the risk. Right now, his enemy was making all the noise, and thereby letting Claridge track him. It was only common sense to watch and wait until he had a fix and he could take down the challenger.

Simple.

He waited, trying to relax, but tension sent involuntary tremors rippling through his body. Claridge reckoned that he wasn't making any noise, and one man couldn't smell another's fear—especially with so much cordite in the air.

His finger curled around the carbine's trigger, taking up the slack. The first warning of danger that his adversary saw would be a muzzle-flash, and bullets would be ripping through his flesh before he had a chance to duck or dodge.

Maybe.

Or, maybe not.

The sounds had stopped. Claridge tried thinking it through,

trying to decide if that was good or bad. Had the guy slipped away, gone to ground, or found a point from which he could drop Claridge with a bullet anytime he felt like it?

Lord, help me!

But the Lord was busy elsewhere, and He offered no reply.

Claridge couldn't wait forever, that was obvious. He'd have to make some kind of move, if only to find out if Cooper was alive. The longer he waited where he was, the more likely it seemed that someone might creep up behind him.

Maybe they were already in place.

The creeper could've served as a diversion.

"At ease, soldier."

Jesus!

The voice came from his left, and Claridge spun in that direction, but his brain took charge before the muscle in his trigger finger got away from him. He didn't have to ask if it was Cooper. There was no one else within a thousand miles who would've sounded quite the same.

"Is that it, then?" he asked instead.

"That's it for now."

"Okay."

Rising, Claridge was once more conscious of his soiled fatigues. Some of the blood and body fluid had been rubbed off on the ground, but he couldn't escape the smell.

"I stink," he said.

"You did all right," Cooper replied.

"I didn't mean—"

"I get it, kid."

"No laundry around here, I suppose."

"Not likely."

"So," he asked, "what do we do?"

"We hurry," Bolan said, and turned away.

8

Garuda Malajit was trying to control himself, but it did not come easily. He watched and listened as Shaitan Takeri told his story for the second time, head wrapped in gauze, voice halting with fatigue, emotion, something.

"I sent out scouts, of course," Takeri was repeating, "but the ambush came completely without warning."

"How is that possible?" asked Malajit, the very picture of serenity.

"I...I'm not sure." The stammer was a sign of something, Malajit supposed. But what? A lie? Exhaustion? Side effects from the head injury? "Perhaps the scouts saw something. They were killed. I know that much."

"It isn't very helpful, though, as you'll agree." Malajit forced a smile, thus amazing himself. "If you had some idea who was responsible, at least..."

"It must have been the army," said Takeri. "Mustn't it?"

"I'm thinking." Icy calm. Where was the rage that Malajit had been expecting ever since Takeri staggered into camp, eyes glazed, one hand clamped to his bleeding head?

Takeri waited, fidgeting on the upturned crate that served him as a seat. Malajit had a folding camp chair, a virtual throne in the primitive camp.

"The guns!" Takeri blurted out.

"What of the guns?"

"They weren't like ours, Kalashnikovs. I heard them. They were lighter caliber. The .223, I'm almost positive."

Malajit shrugged. It proved nothing. Many weapons had adapted to some version of the .223-caliber cartridge favored by America, also known as 5.56 mm. Even the Russian AK-74 was close, with the 5.45 mm round.

"It's strange, still," Malajit remarked.

"What is?" Takeri had a worried look, or was that Malajit's imagination?

"If the army was responsible, why are you still alive? We both know how they operate. The bayonets and head shots for the wounded. Bodies stacked and burned, sometimes. We've both seen it. So, if it was the army, my old friend, why are you here?"

Takeri blinked rapidly, five or six times, then answered with a question of his own. "What if I wasn't there?"

Malajit frowned. "Explain."

"I have the injury, as you're aware." Takeri pointed to his bandage, needlessly. "When consciousness returned to me, I wasn't with the others on the trail. It seems I wandered off some distance from the fight."

"And no one saw you go?"

"There was confusion."

"And a ground force large enough to slaughter your patrol."

"An ambush party. Who can say how many?"

Malajit had reached the point where he had to make a choice. He sensed that Takeri was lying, or holding something back, but he had no idea what it could be. Clearly, the man had not gone out and killed the other members of his own patrol. He never could've managed it, for one thing, as green as they had been. Likewise, he had no motive for betrayal. The Sword of Freedom was his only family.

And yet...

Perhaps it was embarrassment, mingled with fear. Takeri had survived when all his men were killed, escaping with a relatively minor wound. There might be guilt attached to that, though Malajit believed Takeri was immune to such emotions. On the other hand, he might be frightened—rightly so—of Malajit's reaction to the news. It would explain the fidgeting and tentative replies, if he was bracing for a violent fit of rage.

"I see only two choices," Malajit declared, when he had stretched the silence thin enough. "One is to send you back with twice the number of men, to claim our own and find the ambush party. We may yet be avenged."

Takeri was blinking again, eyelids twitching as if in response to some silent alarm signal. "And the other choice?" he asked.

"It's obvious. If you are right, and soldiers are that close, we must break camp and find another place to hide, beyond their reach."

Garuda Malajit knew there was no such place on Borneo. It was an island, after all, with finite possibilities, but he was skilled in the craft of evasion, playing hide-and-seek in a life-or-death league. The government might find him someday, but he didn't think his time had come.

Not yet.

"And so, my friend, what shall it be?"

Takeri didn't blink at him, this time. He stared, dumbfounded, as the choice was left to him.

"You're asking me?"

"Why not? I trust you with my life." Twisting the blade, in case there was some treachery hidden behind those startled eyes.

"Sending another party out so soon," Takeri said, "I worry that the next patrol might lead them here, somehow."

"It's a concern, I grant you."

"If we leave, what of the prisoners?"

"They come with us, of course. I haven't given up on them. They'll serve us yet, in one way or another."

"We could leave them here. As an example to our enemies."

"We could've done that with the ambush party," Malajit replied. "But two gray-haired Americans? It's not so much a message, as a joke."

"Of course." Takeri had no choice but to agree.

"I still have plans for them. You'll see."

"Yes, sir."

"Do you need rest, before we go?"

"No, thank you."

"Right, then. Give the order to break camp. We're going south. I have a place in mind that may be suitable."

Takeri stood up, wobbly on his feet, but he seemed steady enough as he passed from the tent, barking orders to the men. Malajit sat alone on his camp chair, frowning.

Why hadn't he lashed out at Takeri? It would've been easy to strike him, even kill him, but the moment had slipped through his hands without the rush of fury that defined so many other moments in his life.

Maybe I'm getting old, he thought, and turned the frown into a smile.

Not yet.

Thirty-two might be a ripe old age for Third World revolutionaries, but Garuda Malajit still had plans for his life, strategies he meant to carry out before they dropped him in a hole and shoveled dirt on top of him.

He wasn't finished yet, and neither were the two Americans. They had a trek in front of them, and he looked forward to discovering how well they could perform.

AMOS CLARIDGE SAW the Devil's helper coming toward him, grim-faced underneath a bandage that was wrapped around his head, black hair protruding in a kind of greasy topknot. He looked almost comical, but laughing at him could be tantamount to suicide.

He stood before them, hard-eyed, as if daring Claridge or his wife to speak. When they ignored the bait, he said, "We're breaking camp. Be ready to march in half an hour."

Claridge grimaced at the news. He still felt shaky from the beating he'd received. His head still throbbed with pain. His ribs still felt like broken glass.

"Where are we going?" Merilee inquired.

"Be still and do as you are told!" the rebel snapped. "Next time, your punishment won't be so lenient!"

He left them.

"You should sit down," Merilee said. "We still have half an hour. You need rest."

"We both need strength. We need to pray."

"Amos—"

"Don't let these devils test your faith," he cautioned her. "You must be strong."

But Amos Claridge knew he was a hypocrite, because the kidnappers had tested his faith grievously, and he was still afraid that he might fail. Anger, depression and discouragement—he'd felt the full range of emotions verging on despair since they'd been taken from the village murder scene. He had been close to breaking down. Still was, in fact. A forced march might be all it took to finish him.

But he would try to stick it out for Jesus.

And for Merilee.

"I don't believe they'll ever let us go alive," she said. "You can't believe that, Amos."

"I believe God still has plans for us. That's all I need to know. Pray with me. Please."

"Of course."

Kneeling was torture in itself, but Merilee supported him,

then knelt beside him, one arm linked through his. For a moment, Amos feared he would forget the words again, perhaps establish a pattern of failure in the most important aspect of his life, but then it all came flooding back to him.

"Dear Father, hear our plea. We need you now, more than ever before in our lives."

"Amen," said Merilee.

"A grim trial stands before us, Lord. You know that, in your boundless wisdom. We may not be able to succeed and witness your glory without help along the way. Please hear us, Lord."

From Merilee, "Yes, Jesus."

"We ask nothing more, O Father, than to serve you well and in accordance to your plan, whatever that may be. But as your holy scripture says, the flesh is sometimes weak."

"Amen."

It wouldn't hurt to know the plan, of course.

Amos felt a stab of guilt.

It was too much work to stand immediately, so he waited on his knees, with Merilee beside him. All around them, their captors were dismantling tents and making their other gear ready for transport. The camp was such a rudimentary affair, it didn't take them long.

"They're running, Amos. Something has gone wrong."

"It always does, with this sort. The authorities are bound to catch up with them, sooner or later."

"And what if they do? What will happen to us?"

He wanted to say, *We'll be saved,* but Amos knew that might not be the case. He still recalled that couple in the Philippines, a minister shot down by government troops in a rescue attempt, while his wife stood and watched. Then again, if the law got too close, there was nothing to stop their captors from murdering them. Anything to lighten the load.

"I don't know, Merilee," he replied. "It's not for us to see the future laid out plain."

Instead of answering, she said, "I dreamed of Jason last night, Amos."

"Oh?" He'd barely slept and could recall no dreams.

"He's troubled by all this."

"Of course he is. It's only natural."

"I'm worried that he may do something."

"What?" It struck him as ridiculous. "He's in the Navy, Merilee. There's nothing he can do."

"He can be headstrong, even so."

"It was a dream, that's all." Someone had told him, once, that a dream was a wish your heart made. Amos wished he could remember where he'd heard it, but he guessed it didn't matter.

"Just a dream," she echoed, sounding almost disappointed. "Are we finished, then?"

"Not yet," he promised her. "I still believe the Lord has work for us to do, and He won't let us go without a fight."

"I hope you're right," she said. "I don't know how much longer I can wait."

MAHMOUD KENDIK was terrified throughout the helicopter ride, but felt better once he was on the ground. He didn't want to be here, in the middle of the jungle with a government strike force, but there had been no viable alternative. If he'd refused, it would've meant a prison cell, perhaps a bullet in the head. Survival was the first priority.

Out here, at least, he had a fighting chance.

No gun, of course, but he could work on that. There would be moments when his escorts let down their guard, when they were careless. If they met the enemy and triumphed, then there would be surplus weapons for the taking. He could take one, and...

And, what?

The jungle wasn't home, but Kendik reckoned he could always find his way out, if he had the time and means of self-defense. The rebels knew him as a friend, so far, and he would simply be a stranger to the peasants living in their scattered villages around the island. There was no clear reason why they ought to murder him on sight.

It was the Sword of Freedom that concerned him at the moment, more than snakes or spiders, more than quicksand or malaria, more than starvation as he wandered through the forest on his own.

He knew this part of it, somewhat. It's why Major Tripada had selected him to guide the strike team, after all. He'd been to the base camp twice, could've drawn a map of the location for their gunships, but Tripada wanted him to guide the raiders personally.

Fine.

Kendik would do as he was told, it would keep him out of jail and keep the pistol from his head. His dealings with the Sword were strictly business on his part, though he had mouthed their slogans like a true believer in the interest of success. They needn't know he had betrayed them, if they managed to escape the trap.

And if they died, well, that was all the same to him.

The helicopter ride had roughly halved the distance they needed to travel. They could not fly any closer without warning off the very men they came to kill. That was Tripada's logic, and again, no argument had been permitted. Kendik would lead them to the jungle camp, then wait at a safe distance while the strike team did its bloody work.

And if they tried to screw him, they would learn that Mahmoud Kendik still had more than one trick up his sleeve.

Despite the oppressive heat and humidity, the informant wore a long-sleeved camo shirt, with the neck and cuffs tightly buttoned. The cuffs of his trousers were tucked securely into high-topped boots, and a soft hat covered his scalp. With his morbid dread of leeches thus suppressed as far as possible, Kendik made his sweaty way along a narrow track that was neither true path nor game trail, but which was clearly marked for those with eyes to see.

The marks were far from obvious. Last time he'd passed this way, he hadn't blazed the trees like a frontiersman who wants a train of settlers to follow him. Kendik was subtle when it suited him. A nick here and a notched limb there, with random scratchings on a fallen tree and three stones planted in a straight line Nature hadn't drawn. The trail was clear enough to Kendik, but to anyone who didn't know his code—and that group covered everyone on Earth—the signs would be obscure.

Or, so he hoped.

If any of the special forces soldiers following his lead had picked up on the signs, they weren't discussing it. So far, so good. Kendik suspected that his usefulness was limited to pointing them in the direction of their target. If they didn't need him, there'd be no reason why they wouldn't cut his throat and leave him for scavengers.

That would be worse than leeches, he decided, if he had to make a choice.

They still appeared to find him useful, and Kendik would play that hand out to the end. Or almost. The trick was guessing when the end would come, and bailing out before it all came crashing down on top of him.

Kendik had honed brinkmanship to an art form in his own urban environment, running con games and drug scams, fencing stolen merchandise and information, snitching off competitors to the police for fun and profit. He enjoyed the risk, the rush, almost as much as he enjoyed the money.

This was different, of course.

This world was alien to him in ways a foreigner would never understand. The simple fact that he was born and raised on Borneo did not mean he was comfortable in the jungle, climbing mountains, fishing by hand in forest streams, or building thatched huts with half-naked tribesmen. Kendik favored paved streets, reeking alleys, and housing projects crammed to bursting with the desperate poor.

That was his jungle, and he missed it more with every step that took him farther south.

But he could do this job, had to do it, in the interest of survival. If he could deliver the rebels as ordered, without getting killed in the process, he just might have a powerful new friend in the state security service. If nothing else, at least Tripada might leave him alone.

First, though, he had to deliver.

It wouldn't be long now. A few more miles.

Kendik could almost smell the cooking fires.

SHAITAN TAKERI STILL couldn't believe his good fortune. He had pulled it off somehow and saved his own life in the process, without losing anything except his men.

Maybe.

He still imagined that there might be a surprise in store for him. Perhaps Malajit had seen through him and was waiting to get him alone in the jungle, then spring the truth on him before he pulled the trigger or drove a knife between Takeri's ribs.

That image made Takeri wish that he could flee the camp unnoticed, strike off on his own for destinations unimagined, but he couldn't take the risk. All over Borneo, maybe throughout the archipelago, police and special forces officers knew who he was and what he looked like. There were still ways to escape, but without cash and helpful allies it would be a dead-end run to nowhere.

He took heart from the fact that Malajit had broken camp and they were headed south. Taking that step, expending that much energy, meant that some of his story had struck a responsive chord.

And why not? Nearly all of it was true.

His party had been ambushed and annihilated, at least insofar as he knew. Takeri had survived, more by luck than anything else. Granted, the wound he'd self-inflicted with a jagged stone played no part in his salvation, but that had been his only glaring lie.

And Malajit had swallowed it.

Takeri was almost certain.

True certainty would only come a year, five years from now, if Malajit had not exploded into shrieking rage, berating him for his deception in the moment before he stabbed, shot, beat or strangled Takeri to death. Only then could he be positive that he had sold the lie. In the meantime, though, it was a hopeful sign he had not been killed in camp, the first time he had told the story.

Garuda Malajit was not known for his self-restraint. Impulse control was not his strong suit. If he'd known or guessed that Takeri was lying, he should've reacted with furious violence, beyond the control of onlookers. He should've run amok.

Takeri should be dead.

But he wasn't, and what did that mean?

Malajit had trusted him enough to give the travel orders and to see that their captives were ready to march. That was touchy, since Malajit's abuse of the Americans had left them weak. Takeri wasn't sure how far they could travel under their own power, but at least he could get them on the road. If one or both of them collapsed, then Malajit would have a choice to make.

There was a point where complications turned a fair idea

into an ordeal with disastrous consequences. Taking the Americans might not destroy them, but Takeri sensed that it had changed the balance of their situation for the worse. As for his own security, he wasn't sure how much remained, or how much he could trust the men whose cause he shared.

Had they begun to doubt him, since he lost the last patrol? That would undercut his authority as second in command of the Sword. He could retain a measure of respect, perhaps, by brute force and by strength of personality, but not if Malajit also distrusted him. That combination would be fatal.

But he couldn't tell if things had gone that far.

Takeri simply had to wait and see.

The headache he had given to himself still throbbed in time with every footstep, as Takeri made his way along the narrow jungle track, but it was worth the suffering if it had saved his life. The wound would heal, perhaps leaving another scar to please the ladies on one of those rare occasions when the war permitted time for privacy and pleasure.

At the moment, though, it simply hurt.

He'd have to watch the damned flies, too, and make sure none of them got at his wound. The last thing that he needed was maggots feeding on his head.

No, that was wrong.

The very last thing that Takeri needed was for Malajit to realize that he had been deceived.

Maggots were sickening. Garuda Malajit was lethal.

Which brought Takeri to another thought that he had harbored for some time, taking it out now and again to look at, then putting it away to gather dust.

Why should his old friend always be the one in charge?

Takeri didn't crave the duties of command, but if it came down to a choice of life or death with Malajit in charge, Takeri knew which way his vote would go. The others might not follow him, enamored as they were—and terrified, that too—

of Malajit. But if something should happen to their leader—
in the heat of battle, say—then they would almost certainly
accept his second in command as their new leader.

And why not?

It was something to think about, while marching through
the jungle in a drizzling rain, toward yet another camp that
might turn out to be their last.

Whatever else he'd lied about to Malajit, one thing was
true. Someone had slaughtered Takeri's patrol, and those
hunters were probably still in the area, looking for rebels to
kill. Government troops were the most likely suspects, but
Takeri didn't care to give the mystery shooters another chance
at him, no matter who they were.

He only hoped the two Americans wouldn't slow down the
column too much. There was a cure for the problem, if they
did.

All kinds of accidents could happen in the jungle, where
survival of the fittest was the only law in force.

Takeri could almost guarantee it.

MERILEE CLARIDGE concentrated on the simple mechanics of
walking, putting one foot in front of the other. She kept her
right arm linked with her husband's left unless the trail nar-
rowed to a point where they couldn't walk side by side. In that
case, she let Amos lead, the way a righteous husband should.

It let her keep an eye on him.

She worried about his condition, even though he was up
and moving without an audible complaint. The spring was
gone from his step, and he favored the side where his ribs had
been injured. Likewise, from time to time she heard the rasp
of inhalation through his broken nose, but there was nothing
she could do to help.

She wondered if the prayer for strength was helping Amos,
then a pang of guilt cut through her weariness at questioning

the Father. She'd been trained from childhood to accept God's will as inescapable and ultimately beneficial. When her sister died in childhood, when her uncle crashed his pickup truck and landed in a wheelchair, when her parents passed away six months apart—all that had been God's will, the preachers said, and for the best. They couldn't tell her why she should be happy over those events or any of the other private tragedies she'd suffered through the years, but their answer was always the same.

"God works in mysterious ways. We'll understand someday."

Merilee's guilt derived from doubting that there'd ever be an answer she could understand, much less accept. In private moments, recently, she had begun to question not only God's judgment, but His very existence.

That was the crux of it. Of late, she had begun to doubt not only God's sincere intentions and His methods, but also His very existence. That was blasphemy, she realized, and so she'd kept it to herself.

But silence didn't dissipate her doubts.

If anything, they festered with neglect.

Six feet in front of Merilee, her husband lurched and staggered, almost fell. She rushed forward to catch him, and he turned to offer a misshapen smile. "Thank you," he said. "I'm fine. Really."

She could've called him on a commandment violation, lying in the sight of God, but it was not the time or place for argument.

He hadn't fallen yet, and that was something to be thankful for. He wasn't limping badly, though the slight dip to his left was more pronounced than when they'd broken camp, an hour earlier. She didn't know their destination or how far away it was, but she was worried that her husband might collapse somewhere along the way.

What would their captors do, in that case?

It seemed they were valuable enough as hostages to be taken along for the march, instead of being shot and left behind. That should've been good news, but every lagging step she took reminded Merilee that there was no one to meet the ransom demand from their keepers. Those who cared enough to pay couldn't afford it, and the rich man's government was playing games with human pawns from half a world away.

It was enough to make her give up hope.

And yet she hadn't. Not yet, anyway.

But soon, she thought, plodding along the trail. I haven't got much left, Jesus.

In case you're listening.

In case you give a damn.

Merilee half expected a lightning bolt to strike her down, and the image made her smile. In fact, she was close to giggling, hysteria rising, when she swallowed the impulse.

God didn't get involved with his creations any more. Reward and punishment were seemingly passé. People went on about their daily business—lying, stealing, raping, killing—and God ignored them.

The truth, she now suspected, was even worse than a vindictive or sadistic God.

He simply didn't care.

His handmade toys had aged and lost whatever spark of interest they'd once held for Him. He had moved on to something else, newer, more interesting.

And left them all alone to work it out themselves.

All right, then, she decided. That's exactly what I'll do.

9

Bolan paused once an hour on the trail, resting for five minutes while he double-checked his compass bearings. They were still on course.

Another five miles and they should be within sniffing distance of their target. Bolan hoped the patrol they'd wasted hadn't been on a time clock. If they were scouting aimlessly for targets, he should be all right. But if they were supposed to come back at a certain time and missed the deadline, it could trigger new security precautions that would make his job more difficult.

He didn't think about the hostages and what they might be suffering, beyond a hope that they were still alive and fit to travel when he found them. There was no doubt in his mind that he would find them, but predicting their condition was beyond his power.

Bolan hadn't talked about the stats and averages with Jason Claridge. The young man was wound tightly enough as it was, between his parents' abduction and his recent baptism by fire. He didn't need to know that barely one-third of all ransom kidnappings were peacefully resolved, even when payment was delivered on demand. Where ransom was refused, the odds against hostage survival jumped to ninety-eight percent.

Why tell him that, when there was nothing he could do

about it anyway? The job ahead demanded concentration, and the young man was already distracted. Any added pressure, and he might just go ballistic when it wouldn't help.

And if he did? Then, what?

Don't borrow trouble, Bolan warned himself. You've got enough to go around.

Five miles and they would have to scope the rebel camp, locate the hostages and find a means of freeing them that wouldn't land them in the middle of a battle royal. Ideally, Bolan hoped to take them out at night, unnoticed by whatever sentries had the watch, but such plans had a way of going sour, when it counted.

Nice and easy, then, but if the soft probe went to hell, he would be ready with Plan B. And any way he sliced it, Plan B always came out sounding more or less the same.

Scorched earth.

If Bolan couldn't sneak out the captives, he'd have to blast them out. The profiles he'd studied offered little hope that either prisoner would be an asset in a fight. Two missionaries, middle-aged, one of them female, neither trained in any form of self-defense that Washington was able to discover. Bolan didn't know if the were pacifists or fire-and-brimstone types, but they'd been locked up for the best part of a week and likely weren't receiving a high-protein diet.

He expected weakness, trepidation and timidity. The traits that got a hostage killed if he or she had one last shot at freedom but was too feeble or frightened to attempt it. Add the possibility of Stockholm Syndrome, frequently seen among victims of political abductions, and they might even resent him trying to extract them from the rebel camp.

Later he'd talk about that part of it with their son, when they had drawn closer to the target, but he didn't want to waste time. He had a schedule to keep, and the firefight had already cost them precious time.

Bolan didn't bother checking on Claridge, to see if the

SEAL was still keeping pace. He could hear him bringing up the rear, even as quiet as Claridge tried to be. The young man wasn't bad, but he was only human.

And that took Bolan's thoughts in another direction, wondering how Claridge was holding up after his first taste of combat. He didn't seem shaky, but Bolan imagined that the hand-to-hand action had made an impression, as well as leaving bloodstains on his cammies. Claridge had done what he could for the odor, smearing mud and leaf mold over the stains, but he had an air of death about him now that no hot shower in the world could wash away. Having killed another human being with his own hands was inside Claridge now, and Bolan wondered how he'd cope with that.

Long-term, it made no difference to the Executioner, but he didn't want Claridge freezing up five minutes or five hours from now, when the next challenge faced them.

The young man was no good to Bolan or his parents, no good to himself, if he couldn't follow through and do the job for which he'd volunteered. And if he lost it here, he might not be the only one to die.

MAHMOUD KENDIK WAS leading when he found the first corpse on the trail. His party was approaching from upwind, and so it took him by surprise. The dead man lay across his path, facedown, legs splayed. One arm was trapped beneath the body, and the other raised above the dead man's head, as if he'd been cut down while summoning a taxi.

Kendik stopped and raised a hand to keep the special forces men from bumping into him. The nearest of them crowded forward, cautiously, and peered over his shoulders at the body.

"Not a regular," one of them said.

Kendik already knew that, from the clothes the dead man wore. The shirt and trousers didn't match, for one thing:

bloodied camouflage above and simple olive drab below. His shoes were split-toed sandals, probably homemade, with soles cut from old truck tires. His bandolier was threadbare khaki, and the magazines that spilled from one torn pouch were made to fit an AK-47.

"A rebel," one of the insightful special forces men decided.

"More than one," Kendik informed him, moving slowly forward to survey the battleground. He had the smell of death and cordite in his nostrils now, nothing the breeze could do to trick him when they were this close.

He counted eleven bodies scattered over forty yards before he gave up, leaving the rest to his companions. They found four more in the brush flanking the narrow trail, while Kendik watched them from the far end of the slaughter ground.

"All rebels," said the sergeant who commanded the patrol. "None of our own."

"Your people didn't kill them," Kendik said.

The sergeant frowned at him, and then said, "No."

That much was obvious. Official hunters would've searched the bodies, turned their pockets inside out or maybe stripped them, and their weapons would've been collected on the spot. The dead surrounding Kendik had not been touched, aside from the infliction of their fatal wounds. Most of them had weapons close at hand.

For all the good that they had done.

Kendik wasted no time trying to guess who'd ambushed the guerrillas, and the why of it held no compelling interest for him.

"They're all dead here," the sergeant said, a moment later. "How much farther to the camp?"

"We should be there by nightfall," Kendik estimated.

"Good. See that we are." As if the order could remove all obstacles they might encounter on the last leg of their trek.

"We'd best be going, then," said Kendik, turning from the dead and setting off once more along the southbound track.

He didn't know what the soldiers were feeling, but his own mood hovered somewhere between agitation and dread. Kendik reckoned there was no great risk of another ambush nearby, but he couldn't be sure. The killers of those fifteen men might still be lurking in the forest close at hand, or moving toward the same camp he'd been drafted to expose.

Kendik had no desire to meet them, but he recognized that it could open up a world of possibilities. If he was not killed in the first few seconds after one group met the other, maybe he could slip away, unnoticed, and escape.

Maybe.

But one way or another, Mahmoud Kendik didn't plan on dying for the government.

Not if they gave him any choice at all.

AN HOUR PAST the firefight, Jason Claridge started winding down. Or maybe crashing would've been a better term for what he felt. One moment, he was moving through the jungle in a state of high alert; the next, he felt as if someone had pulled a plug and let the pent-up tension bleed out through his feet, into the earth.

He didn't know if that was good or bad, but Claridge wasn't letting down his guard. He still wore splotches of a stranger's blood and other things that weren't supposed to see the light of day, and that was all he needed in the way of a reminder that his mission could result in sudden death.

I need to stay alive. Please, Jesus.

Claridge wondered if it would be blasphemous to pray for the destruction of his enemies. Old Testament heroes had done it all the time, seeing their faith rewarded as they slaughtered tens of thousands in God's name. But times had obviously changed. Today, the talking heads on television would've called it genocide, and the United Nations likely would've passed a resolution to condemn it. Washington might organize a coalition to restore the peace, especially if there were oil fields in the neighborhood.

But God would always triumph.

It was carved in stone.

The question that tormented Claridge was whether he had done God's will by going AWOL to retrieve his parents, or if he had placed himself unwittingly in opposition to the Lord. If so, he literally didn't have a hope in hell.

He'd prayed all night before making his choice, and there'd been no sign warning him to stay away. Of course, that wasn't proof that God approved of his decision. Messages from the Almighty were uncommon at the best of times, and they were often subtle. Claridge guessed he might've overlooked one, in his haste to act.

If so, then he was screwed.

A foot-long lizard scuttled up the trunk of a tree to his left, making Claridge flinch before he recognized the source of sudden motion at his side. The reptile turned its head and eye-balled him, then vanished into foliage with another burst of speed.

Cooper had gained a few yards while Claridge was distracted. The young man picked up his pace, being careful about it, yet knowing he couldn't afford to let Cooper get too far ahead. Claridge still didn't know where they were going, beyond a generally southerly direction, and he guessed he could follow that course to the sea without finding his parents, unless he stuck with his reluctant guide.

Was *that* the sign?

Claridge thought about it, trying to calculate the odds of a coincidental meeting with this stranger in the wilds of Borneo. Not just a soldier, but one who'd been sent to rescue his parents at the very same moment Claridge was bent on doing the same. It seemed to Claridge that the odds against such a chance encounter must be astronomical. Billions or trillions to one sounded right.

Did that make it a miracle?

Claridge wasn't even sure what that meant, anymore. People used the word so often it had lost its wonder.

But meeting Cooper, out of all the people in the world, and on Borneo, no less…

Well, maybe.

Whatever it was, God's work or dumb coincidence, Claridge didn't plan to look this particular gift horse in the mouth. He wasn't about to let Cooper lose him in the jungle, or to flinch from any trial along the way. If he had to face a horde of demons and wade through their blood to rescue his parents, that's what he'd do. Claridge was hanging on to the end of the line, whatever that meant.

And God help anyone who got in his way.

"THIS IS THE PLACE," Garuda Malajit declared. Spread out around him, soldiers burdened with equipment eyed the forest clearing where he'd called them to a halt, checking its strong and weak points as a new base camp.

Malajit would be the first to say it wasn't perfect. But, then, what was? They had a stream nearby for water, and the clearing was surrounded by giant trees that kept it shaded unless the sun was directly overhead, beaming down through a fifty-foot hole in the canopy.

He stepped into the center of the clearing, with the hole one hundred feet above him. "Set up the tents on the perimeter," he ordered. "Avoid the point where I stand now, and you'll be hidden well."

That wasn't strictly true, he realized. A helicopter fitted with thermal-imaging equipment could spot men, vehicles and campfires by their heat, regardless of leaves in the way, but Indonesian soldiers were not skilled at using such sophisticated toys. The gear only seemed to work properly if American advisers went along for the ride. Otherwise, the helicopter pilots flew broad circles over virgin jungle and returned to say they'd found nothing beyond some villages already on the map.

Malajit knew all that because he had a friend or two inside the army, serving as his eyes and ears in the enemy camp. He also knew his opposition well enough to recognize their natural laziness and corruption. Most of his adversaries didn't mind killing defenseless civilians, or shooting rebels from a distance with artillery or flying gunships, but they had little taste for close combat on the ground. They would avoid an all-out battle if they could, and live to loaf another day.

This time it could be different. Malajit had raised the ante by grabbing the two Americans, insignificant as they were to their own government. Their abduction had stiffened the spines of his foes, at least a little, while they tried to save face in the eyes of the world. Still, a lifetime of sloth could not be reformed in a week or a month.

If he gave them a way to *not* find him, Garuda believed, most of the soldiers hunting him would gladly seize the opportunity to let him go.

And if he was wrong…well, then he might surprise them with the strength and sheer ferocity of his resistance when they came for him.

He thought about the prisoners and felt the old, familiar anger welling up. Malajit had not been certain they'd survive the march, but both had staggered to the end. Granted, they had required some not-so-gentle prodding as they went along, but both of them were still alive, damn it.

The jungle hadn't solved his problem for him, which meant Malajit would have to think of something else.

A bullet was the quickest way. Two seconds for the execution, and his men could dump them somewhere in the jungle, well beyond the camp. If someone found their bones a decade or a century from now, what difference would it make to history?

But then, he thought, a different way might be to give them back.

Frowning, watching his men pitch camp, he turned the problem over in his mind. Other guerrilla bands had freed hostages at one time or another, without collecting ransom. Sometimes it was a sympathy ploy, as when one of the prisoners was ill and needed help that couldn't be provided in captivity. In other situations, Malajit recalled, freedom had been exchanged for amnesty. The kidnappers admitted a mistake and freed their captives, while the other side called off their hunting dogs, at least for the time being.

Malajit knew he could not confess to an error. His opponents were corrupt and cruel savages in uniforms and business suits. If Malajit professed that *he* was wrong, that he'd misled the Sword of Freedom, it would tell the world his enemies were decent, honest men. It would shame Malajit— and, equally important, it would not prevent the other side from hunting him. They'd simply lie about it to the media and then go on behaving any way they chose, secure in their ability to manage daily "news."

So much for freeing the Americans.

A second avenue, denying any role in the kidnapping plot, was likewise closed to him. His mouthpiece in Jakarta had been too effective on that score for Malajit to reverse himself now and claim it was all a mistake. Even if he hadn't kidnapped the Americans, but simply took credit for someone else's act, he was now on the hook for that crime.

Fuming, he considered the short list of remaining options. Surrender was unthinkable. Before his enemies were finished with him, he'd be praying for the mercy of a firing squad. Escape from Borneo would be so difficult that Malajit rated it next to impossible.

That left two choices.

He could execute the prisoners and keep on trying to dodge his pursuers, or he could seek to reopen the negotiations.

But with whom?

It was a problem to consider when his mood had stabilized. Malajit felt a need to vent his anger. Perhaps he could find a sloppy soldier in camp who'd done a poor job setting up his tent.

Hopeful, he went in search of prey.

"THEY'RE GONE?" Jason Claridge asked, speaking through clenched teeth. "How can that be?"

"They left," Bolan replied. "Pulled up and left."

"But—"

"No buts," Bolan interrupted him. "We need to find their trail ASAP."

There was no doubt he'd had the right coordinates. The hacked-out clearing spread before him had been someone's camp, and very recently. The marks of cooking fires were plain to see, and Bolan's nostrils told him where to look for the latrines, off to his left among the trees. His quarry had done well at picking up the pieces of their fugitive existence in a hurry, but he still found other signs to mark their passing. Rope scars on some of the trees, where tents or cammo nets had been supported. Freshly turned earth, where they'd buried their trash. A flurry of gashes on one giant tree trunk where someone had passed the time throwing knives.

He couldn't see anything that denoted the presence of two prisoners. Claridge scoured the clearing, but Bolan knew he was wasting his time. The SEAL hadn't seen his parents in months. He'd have no idea what they were wearing, how to recognize their footprints on the clearing's trampled ground, or what a clue would look like if they'd had a chance to leave one.

He could've told Claridge to look for graves, but Bolan didn't think the hostages were dead. If they'd been executed, he believed their captors would've left the bodies on display for any visitors to find. Showing the world what happened when their ransom demands were rejected. An absence of bodies told Bolan the hostages were likely still living, though he wouldn't want to speculate on their condition.

"No sign of them," said Claridge, from the far side of the clearing.

"Find the trail," Bolan repeated. "It's the only way you'll ever find them."

"Right. Okay."

The trouble with a long-term camp was that its occupants went off in all directions, day by day, and beat the shrubbery down each time they passed. He'd have to judge whatever trail they chose to follow on the basis of its size, how fresh it was, and where it seemed to lead. They could waste hours, maybe days, if Bolan chose the wrong path.

One bonus, working in the jungle, was that plants returned to claim their turf as soon as humans turned their backs. A month from now, the clearing would be overgrown, most of the signs left by the men he hunted either buried or erased. The freshest, largest trail that they could find retreating from the camp, most likely headed farther south, would be the one to take.

He found it while Claridge was scouting the eastern perimeter, taking off on short side trips into the forest. It wasn't quite a highway, but Bolan saw the way ferns and undergrowth had been trampled flat by two or three persons traveling abreast, with enough of them following behind to make the damage semipermanent.

How many?

From the camp's size and the evidence before him, Bolan guessed that they were talking seventy or eighty rebels altogether.

"Got it," he told Jason Claridge, waiting at the edge of the forest until the young man joined him.

"Are you sure?"

"I'm sure."

"Okay. What now?"

"We follow them," Bolan replied. "And hope they don't feel a need to lighten their load in a hurry."

THREE HOURS LATER, Mahmoud Kendik stood in the clearing and told his companions, "Gone. We're too late."

"For this spot, maybe," the sergeant informed him, "but not for the chase."

"This is the place I knew," Kendik replied. "I can't say where they'll go from here."

The sergeant smiled at that. "Nobody's asking you," he said. "You got us here. We'll do the rest."

The feeling that came over Kendik started as relief, then veered toward panic. If they didn't need him anymore, what would prevent them killing him, or leaving him alone to find his way out of the jungle in his own good time?

"If you don't need me," he began, but never had the chance to finish it.

"You're going with us," said the sergeant, cutting off any debate. "It's safer that way."

"Safer?"

"I have orders. You will not be freed to warn your friends that we are looking for them. You're in custody, in case the fact had slipped your mind."

"I've not forgotten it."

"I hope not. Should you wander off by accident, somewhere along the trail, you will be shot."

"Threats are unnecessary, Sergeant."

"Then consider it a warning, and be quiet while we find which way they went."

He left them to it, sat down in the middle of the clearing and observed the special forces soldiers moving here and there with perfect discipline. He guessed they had some skill in tracking, though it would've served him better if they hadn't. That way, the sergeant would have to relent and they could all go back to civilization.

What waited for him there?

Kendik wasn't sure, but he liked his chances better in the city, even under scrutiny, than trekking through the jungle toward a firefight on some godforsaken battleground. He had the pistol, still unnoticed by his escorts, but it wouldn't count for much in a pitched battle between determined enemies.

Not much, but perhaps just enough.

The key, if they overtook the rebels, was for Kendik to avoid any contact with Garuda Malajit or Shaitan Takeri. Both would instantly regard him as a traitor, and they wouldn't hesitate to kill him if the opportunity arose. Rather than face that possibility, even with stolen gun in hand, Kendik preferred to avoid killing conflicts as long as he could.

Escape was still an option, but the sergeant and his men watched Kendik closely, tracking him with wary eyes each time he made a move. One of them followed him when nature called, and it would not be easy to outwit them here, on ground they knew better than he did. Perhaps if they found Malajit's people, and battle was joined, he'd have a better chance of slipping through the net and vanishing while they were otherwise engaged.

Perhaps.

If not, he simply had to wait and hope the sergeant's soldiers were victorious. He had a better chance of getting back alive with them, than if they fell before the Sword of Freedom.

The men with whom he'd once done business would be merciless. That much, Kendik knew beyond the shadow of a doubt. He'd seen the way they handled even minor treachery, an incident involving theft of food that ended gruesomely, with screams.

He didn't want to think about that now, could not afford to let the images seep through and dominate his thoughts. Mahmoud Kendik needed to stay alert, be ready when—

"I've found it!"

He turned toward the sound of the loud, disgustingly cheerful voice. A corporal stood on the southern edge of the clearing, smiling as he pointed off into the trees.

"They went this way!" the young soldier told them.

"Let's see," said the sergeant, crossing to the spot and moving on a short distance into the forest. He returned a moment later, nodding in agreement. "Well done, Corporal. It's this way, definitely. Quickly now, two point men. You and you! Single file, the rest of you, behind them."

Kendik fell in line without complaint. He would gain nothing by creating problems at the moment, but he might yet benefit by cultivating the sergeant's goodwill. For all his suspicion, the patrol's leader would be distracted soon enough, should they overtake their quarry. When that happened, Kendik didn't want a single fragment of the sergeant's consciousness consumed with him, when there were more important things to do.

Like staying alive, and killing the enemy.

Mahmoud Kendik might have his chance yet.

If he could only watch and wait.

10

Shaitan Takeri knew he should've seen it coming. Malajit had been too calm as he listened to the ambush story, thinking of his soldiers lying slaughtered in the forest. Someone had to pay for that, and in the absence of an enemy, Takeri was the logical candidate.

Still, it could've been worse.

Malajit might have killed him, or ordered his death, instead of simply assigning Takeri to this jungle rear-guard action in defense of the retreating column. All Takeri really had to do was watch and wait for anyone who might be following the party.

And kill them. Yes, that too.

He'd been assigned five men to help him do that job, if it proved necessary. The number told Takeri that Malajit took the order seriously, doubtless thinking of the men he had already lost, determined not to let an unknown enemy pursue him to his new stronghold. Takeri hoped no one would come along the trail to fight, or if they did, that there would only be a few of them.

He'd lost more than a dozen men already. Five more gave him little comfort as the jungle shadows closed around him, the afternoon shifting toward night.

Takeri wasn't frightened. Not the way he had been in the ambush, when the world had blown up in his face. But it would've been fair to say he was concerned. It wouldn't take the greatest woodsman on the planet to follow the trail their party had left while retreating. He wouldn't say a child could follow it, but any competent hunter could track them with ease.

And they were being hunted. That much he knew.

The generals in Jakarta had placed a bounty on his head, and a larger one on Malajit's, for the trouble they'd caused on Borneo. Soldiers were ineligible for the payoff, meaning that the bounty was supposed to turn peasants against them, encouraging spies to come forward with names and addresses.

It hadn't worked so far, but the plan only needed one informer to put the wheels in motion. Had someone tipped off the soldiers to their campsite, or was the earlier clash a simple coincidence? Takeri didn't know and had no way of finding out. If there was someone squealing to the authorities, he ought to find out who the traitors were and punish them, but he had no such power at the moment. And, if he was honest with himself, the candidates were far too numerous for him to single out the guilty ones.

Takeri had staked out his men in a modified ambush position, to cover the trail. The two forward observers were stationed one hundred yards out from his own position, flanking the path that he assumed their enemies would follow, if and when they came. Two more lay waiting at the fifty-yard mark, to cover their comrades and to pick off any adversaries who got past the point men. Finally, Takeri and his fifth man waited at the end of the gauntlet, to finish any stragglers who escaped the first four guns.

With any luck at all, he wouldn't have to fire a shot.

The worst part of his present duty was that he'd been left without communications gear. He couldn't check his men, make sure they were awake and on alert, unless he went to them. Better to take his chances, he'd decided, after pointedly reminding them about the friends they'd lost in the last forest skirmish.

If that didn't sharpen their senses, Takeri couldn't think of anything that would. And he didn't feel like creeping through the jungle every half hour or so to check on his people, taking their monotonous reports that nothing had happened. Takeri knew that already. He could hear it not happening, all around him.

If only—

The first shot made him jump, clutching his AK-47 to his chest and almost triggering a burst on reflex. Beside him, the young guerrilla glanced at Takeri, then turned his eyes back to the trail before them, as more firing erupted, muzzle-flashes winking in the jungle dusk.

So much for luck.

Takeri watched and waited, looking for a target.

Seeking someone he could kill.

THE FIRST SHOT had been close, Bolan would give them that. If the sniper had set his Kalashnikov for full-auto-fire, instead of single shots, he might've gotten lucky with the third or fourth rounds, after the first one whistled over Bolan's head.

Too late for that.

Bolan was down and under cover by the time the other shooters opened up, all firing automatic now. He glanced back toward Claridge, or where the SEAL should've been, but there was no trace of him.

Fair enough.

Every man for himself.

The trap had been well set, his adversaries well concealed. They had been nearly good enough, or maybe Bolan had begun to take the trail for granted, moving through the forest in a kind of mental autopilot mode. Charting the progress of his quarry, when he should've watched more closely for a snare.

It was an error, right, but not a fatal one.

Not yet.

Rather than instantly returning fire, he started circling to his right, crawling beneath the bursts of 7.62 mm slugs that flayed the undergrowth three feet above him. He didn't want to give his enemies a target, until he knew that he could make his first shots count.

Somewhere behind him and away to Bolan's left, he heard Claridge lay down a short burst from his CAR-15. It drew attention from the place where Bolan made his creeping way along the forest floor, still covering whatever sounds he made as four or five AKs replied in kind. He hoped Claridge was covering himself, but there was nothing he could do about it now.

Bolan was ninety seconds into it before he caught the first glimpse of a target. It was only one man, but he had to start somewhere.

The shooter had good cover, crouching in the shadow of one giant tree, partly protected by a smaller one on his left flank. Had a decent field of fire along the trail, northward, and from the sounds of gunfire up ahead, his back was covered by at least one other rifleman.

Bolan could see him, though, a wedge of head and shoulder moving back and forth between the intervening trees and shrubbery. It might not be the best shot he had ever taken, but it wouldn't be the worst, either.

Too risky for the Glock, Bolan decided. A muffled shot was safer in the circumstances, but it would be wasted if he couldn't put his target down. Instead, he edged a little closer to the mark and found an angle for the Steyr's optical sight, bringing the sniper's head and shoulders into clear relief.

Bolan held steady on his mark, expelled his breath and squeezed the trigger lightly. Three rounds rattled off in two-tenths of a second. One of them missed, shaving bark from a tree, while the other two drilled flesh and bone, pitching the sniper face first to the ground.

Bolan was moving by the time it registered on anybody else, scrabbling through ferns and over twisted tree roots, wishing he could make himself invisible. The jungle helped, but one of the shooters still came too close for comfort, bullets chiseling an abstract pattern into bark a foot above Bolan's rump.

He froze, a gamble in itself, since he didn't know if the gunman was lucky or gifted. Lucky meant the near miss could've been coincidence. Gifted would mean he had a deadly eye and might've picked up Bolan's movements, could be sighting in the kill right now.

Bolan waited, then relaxed a little as the next rounds swept past him, probing the shadows away to his right.

Call it lucky.

He had another choice to make. Should he proceed along the trail, taking the shooters out on this side where he could, or double back and find the one paired with the sniper he'd just dropped? Help Claridge out, or let him pull his weight?

Move on.

The Executioner crept forward, following the sounds of gunfire toward his prey.

JASON CLARIDGE HUGGED the great tree that had saved his life by absorbing half a dozen AK-47 bullets meant for him, and wondered whether this would be the end.

He hadn't seen the ambush coming, nearly lost it when the first shots echoed through the jungle stillness, and he'd come close to firing back before he had a decent target in his sight.

No target yet, in fact, though one of the concealed snipers had obviously seen him well enough to come within a foot or so of dropping him.

Snap out of it!

His parents needed him, and he'd be no good to them rotting in the jungle with a bullet in his head.

Instinctively he knew they hadn't found the enemy's main force. Matt Cooper would've known if they were that close to another camp. Claridge had seen him work and trusted him to that extent.

Cooper had missed the ambush, though, a human failing after all. And was he still alive?

Oh, God, what if he's dead?

In that case, Claridge would be back where he started, tracking his parents' kidnappers alone, but knowing roughly where to look for them.

If he got past this test alive.

More bullets raked the tree where he was crouched, concealed, and Claridge knew a lunge into the open would be suicidal. Instead of revealing himself, he unclipped a frag grenade from his web belt, scanning his memory for its best impression of his enemy's position.

He'd been running, seeking cover, but the muzzle-flash had registered in peripheral vision. Claridge estimated that the shooter must be forty-odd feet to his right, call it thirty degrees off center as he faced due south. He'd have to make the pitch left-handed, but he trained for that, the moves ingrained in muscle memory.

He pulled the pin and dropped it, waiting for the next burst of fire to sweep past him before he made the toss. It came and went, with Claridge right behind it, putting everything he had into the looping sidearm throw. Counting the seconds as the little bomb was airborne, arcing toward its target.

He was ready for the blast, muted by forest greenery and gunfire as if someone had thrown a blanket over the grenade before it blew. To judge the accuracy of his pitch, Claridge had to expose himself, and there was no time like the present if he meant to make a move.

Low and outside, he lunged through space, leaving the tree's shelter behind him, landing on his belly in what looked like mud and smelled like dung. He had his CAR-15 leveled in the direction of the blast, ready to fire at anything that moved unless it wore Matt Cooper's face.

A man was rising, lurching from the smoky bushes. He didn't look like Cooper, smaller all around, and Claridge gave him three rounds to the chest despite his empty, dangling hands.

Kill or be killed.

Right now, it was the only game in town.

The next shooter was tracking him, already tearing up the landscape with his Kalashnikov. Claridge rolled and slithered, doing everything they'd taught him, praying it was good enough. A yard or less behind him, bullets kicked up spurts of turf and hacked the undergrowth to tatters.

Claridge could see the muzzle-flash—one of them, anyway. There might be others he was missing, that would smother him with fire when he responded to the first, but he would have to take that chance. One of the surest ways to die in combat was by simply doing nothing.

Claridge found his mark and held it long enough to stroke the carbine's trigger twice. Six rounds away, no tracers in the magazine to reassure him that his aim was true.

Lord, help me!

Was it wrong to pray for help in killing other men? He didn't know, but it was an instinctive reflex, drilled into his head and heart from infancy.

When you were in trouble, talk to God.

He was in trouble now, but Claridge wasn't sure that God had anything to do with it. His recklessness had brought him here.

And loyalty. Maybe the Lord gave points for that.

Claridge lay waiting for the sniper to return fire, but it didn't happen. Could it be that easy, taking down his second adversary?

Easy, right. Like falling in a grave.

The other shooters found him then, and Claridge banished any thoughts of God, his parents, or the life he'd left behind. The only thing that he had time to think about was killing, and the primal urge to stay alive.

SHAITAN TAKERI KNEW he couldn't run this time. If he lost another squad and ran away, he'd have to flee the country to escape Garuda Malajit's wrath. And if Malajit or his agents caught up with Takeri, there would be nothing quick or clean about his death.

Better to fight where he was, as his manhood demanded, and do his utmost to destroy his enemies.

And still, he hadn't fired his weapon yet.

There was a method to his strange procrastination. Takeri had ordered his companion forward, leaving the plug position of their ambush, circling around the left flank, while he crept forward on the right. He had not fired because he had no target yet, just muzzle-flashes in the dusk. He could distinguish weapons by their sounds, but in the general confusion of the firefight Takeri was frightened of shooting his own men by mistake.

The first grenade blast startled him and almost made Takeri run. His men had no grenades, which told him they were overmatched. He didn't know how many adversaries, though he marked the sounds of hostile guns from at least two locations.

Why not massed firing?

His mind ticked off the possibilities. A scouting party, perhaps, surprised to meet his soldiers? Bandits passing through the territory, heedless of political events?

Takeri didn't buy the notion of coincidence, after his first bloody encounter with the faceless enemy, but answers were less important now than solutions to his immediate problem.

He had to kill these strangers, and he had to do it soon. Each moment wasted gave them another chance to whittle his ranks, or to summon untold reinforcements to the battle scene. In either case, speed mattered.

It was all the more maddening, then, that Takeri's fear made him proceed at a snail's pace through the jungle, creeping on his belly and freezing every time a shot rang out or something rustled past him in the undergrowth. He half expected enemies to leap out from the shadows and surround him as he crawled along the muddy ground, despite his understanding that they were in front of him, still battling with his men.

Takeri's own sweat was rank in his nostrils. It stank of fear, and he wondered whether he could ever wash away that smell. If it would mark him as a coward for the rest of his days.

Pushing through a screen of ferns, Takeri gasped at the sight of a face mere inches from his own. The eyes were locked open, staring into his, but they were sightless in death. A heartbeat later, he recognized the young man as a member of his rear-guard squad, though he could not recall a name.

It was too late to chastise him in any case, for shirking on the job. A bullet or shard of shrapnel had torn through the dead man's throat and silenced him forever, as it severed the lifeline to his lungs. From the expression on that face, it wasn't clear if died instantly or lay gasping in vain for breath he couldn't draw.

What difference did it make?

He was out of the fight, one less gun on Takeri's side of the skirmish. The odds in his favor had just been decreased, and he still didn't know what they were.

Takeri detoured around the corpse, breathing through his mouth to minimize the smell of blood and death that already enveloped the body. When he had progressed a yard or so beyond it, Takeri saw a shadow figure moving through the semi-darkness up ahead. He couldn't make out any features of the stalker's face or uniform, but the man was coming in his direction, stealthy movements covered by the sounds of gunfire all around.

Takeri wasn't sure, but he'd come within a stone's throw of where he supposed the frontlines had to be. Who else but an enemy would be creeping back toward his position through the trees, as if stalking prey?

Takeri triggered a burst from his AK-47 and saw the shadow stagger. Incredibly, it was still lurching toward him, arms flailing now as it tried to stay upright.

He fired again, burning up half a magazine in his panic, and the target collapsed, to lie twitching on the ground.

He rushed forward, digging with knees and elbows to reach his kill—then froze, as he recognized the face. Even with half of it shot away, Takeri knew the soldier he'd assigned to one of the key point positions.

His mind was racing, swirling, when he heard a sound beside him, on his right. Turning his head, Takeri squinted at the object that had fallen from thin air.

He recognized a hand grenade.

MAHMOUD KENDIK FROWNED at the sound of the second explosion, gunfire still echoing through the jungle from a distance. He couldn't say with any confidence how far away the battle was. Sounds seemed to carry farther in the dark, for some reason.

The shooting meant that they were now on hostile ground, no doubt about it any longer. Kendik had briefly fooled himself into thinking they might be safe, that they could wander around through the forest for another day or so and then give up the search, without ever finding the killers they sought.

The gunfire and explosions killed that dream.

Not only did they mark the forest as a war zone, but they

also gave his special forces escorts a fix on the direction they should travel. Already, the sergeant was muttering orders, reminding the others that speed and caution were not incompatible concepts. They could hurry without being reckless, make time without blundering into at trap.

Or, could they?

Kendik was worried that the soldiers might be overestimating their abilities. He understood that elite fighting units encouraged cocky gung-ho attitudes, and while he wouldn't care to tangle with any of the commandos around him, they were only flesh and blood. A well-placed blade or bullet would drop any one of their number, as quickly as it would some untutored lout in the slums.

Kendik hoped their inflated self-confidence wouldn't be the death of him.

Still, he had no choice but to accompany the soldiers, as they set off toward the sounds of battle. There was a limit to their haste, imposed by the surroundings. The jungle night was treacherous, too many hidden snares for them to double-time over hostile ground, but Kendik felt them straining toward the action, emitting a feral odor of aggression that must be the counterpart of fear.

He knew about the fight-or-flight reflex, and guessed that flight had been eradicated from the mind-set of these fighting men. They lived for combat, lusted after it as most men lust for women, spurred on by gunpowder aphrodisiacs. Killing was second nature to this lot.

He only hoped that their survival skills were equally fine-tuned. His destiny was linked to theirs, unless he could somehow escape.

That seemed unlikely at the moment, as they forged ahead through forest undergrowth that clutched and snagged Kendik's clothing like fingers, trying to draw him aside from the trail. He pushed that image out of mind, refusing to indulge in the superstitious nonsense that so many of his people held dear. The only evil spirits in this jungle, Kendik told himself, were those marching around him and the ones they'd come to kill.

All of a kind, they were, in his opinion. It was simply his bad luck that he'd been nabbed while dealing with the rebels and was now ensnared in their bloody politics.

Ensnared, perhaps—but not done, yet.

He marched, quickstepping through the jungle, stumbling now and then. It was tough going, but Kendik also exaggerated his own clumsiness. When it was time for him to fall, or lurch off to one side, he wanted the move to seem natural, part of his staggering progress along the faint trail.

They were gaining on the sounds of battle, but not swiftly enough to suit the commandos who surrounded him. Kendik could hear them huffing from frustration, as much as from the sheer exertion of their march. They were keyed up for killing.

He knew they'd gladly start with him if he made any unexpected moves.

THE GRENADE BLAST sent shrapnel zipping through the jungle greenery. Bolan ducked in time to save his face from razor-edged shards that sliced across the tree beside him, leaving ragged claw marks on the bark.

He wasn't sure if that was Claridge pitching, or the opposition, but a shrapnel hit would have the same impact, regardless of who pulled the pin. He didn't fire immediately, waiting to see what came of the blast, tracking sounds in the bush that told him someone was disoriented, maybe wounded, and about to panic.

When the target staggered into view, it wasn't Jason Claridge. Bolan didn't recognize the Asian face, but the AK-47 dangling limply from one of the newcomer's hands told him everything he had to know about this one. A 3-round burst from the Steyr AUG dropped the man in his tracks, and Bolan moved past him.

A couple of AKs were still in the fight, one away to his right, the other more or less in front of him. If they had concrete targets, Bolan wasn't one of them, their bullets flying high and wide. He stayed below their line of fire, probing the shadows that had lowered to near-darkness now, exacerbated by another drizzling rain.

Life and death in the jungle.

So, what else was new?

Another burst of 5.56 mm fire, echoing from his right flank, boosted Bolan's confidence that Claridge was still fit for action. The hostiles were all using AKs, as far as he knew, so he still had a friend in the fight—if Claridge didn't spook and shoot him by mistake.

One of the two Kalashnikovs was closer now, still laying down sporadic bursts of fire. Bolan had no idea what the gunner was doing, or what he hoped to accomplish by spraying the forest without a clear mark, but the sounds served as homing beacons for the Executioner, moving in for the kill.

He crawled the last ten yards or so, coming in from the shooter's left and staying well below the odd bursts fired in his general direction. He was close enough now to hear the sounds of reloading as the rifleman switched magazines, and Bolan seized the moment, erupting from cover to rush the enemy position, leading with his AUG.

The shooter heard Bolan coming, then saw him. Too late. He had the AK's magazine jammed somehow, maybe fumbling in haste, and when he tried to rack the slide nothing happened.

Bolan triggered three rounds from the hip and knocked his adversary sprawling. The guy still had some life left in him, squirming like a beached catfish, but Bolan pitched his rifle out of reach and waited, listening to the forest.

Bolan understood a second burst from the Steyr could mark him for the gunman still out there and fighting. He would've spared the dying man a mercy round, but with survival on the line, he was as hard and cold as stainless steel.

The problem solved itself a moment later, when the dying rebel coughed and shivered out the final spasms of his life. Bolan stayed where he was, reading the momentary silence of the forest, knowing there was still a mortal risk if he got careless.

Someone was moving, and being none too subtle in the process. Bolan had a fix and had begun to track the unseen shooter's progress, when another blaze of gunfire lit the darkened jungle.

Two men were firing, one with a Kalashnikov, the other one—he hoped—a CAR-15. They traded close-range bursts for several seconds, then a ragged cry of pain wafted to Bolan's ears, and silence reigned once more.

Bolan shifted to his right, as quietly as possible, and settled down behind the solid body of a fallen tree. It was the best cover available, and still might not protect him from incoming fire, but Bolan knew he had to risk it, had to break the silent stalemate.

Staying low, he called out softly, "Claridge?"

"Here!" the voice came back.

When no one fired at either of them, Bolan guessed that they were clear. He rose, still cautious, finger ready on the AUG's hair-trigger as he waited for the SEAL to show himself.

"I'm coming over," Claridge told him.

"Come ahead."

The young man bore a vague resemblance to the soldier who'd been tracking Bolan through the bush, just a day before. A lifetime had elapsed since then, for several of their enemies, but they were still alive.

"Are you all right?" he asked Claridge.

"Still kicking."

"Good. We're running late."

"Who were these guys?" asked Claridge.

"Probably a rear-guard. We've got someone worried."

"So, they know we're coming?"

"They know someone's coming after them. That's why they're running, leaving traps along the way. They won't know who, exactly."

Claridge turned his grim face south, in the direction of their interrupted march. "What if they spook and kill my parents?"

"It's a risk," Bolan confirmed. "We can't do anything about it, standing here."

"Okay," the SEAL replied. "What are we waiting for?"

11

Garuda Malajit was getting nervous. He wished, now, that he had supplied Shaitan Takeri with a two-way radio, to stay in contact with the ambush party, but he only had two sets in camp and hadn't felt that they could spare one. At the same time, he admitted this much to himself, he'd hoped that being isolated in the jungle with another small patrol would serve as partial punishment for Takeri's loss of the first squad.

Now, the Sword of Freedom's leader had begun to doubt himself. He was becoming anxious, and his well-known tics unnerved his men. They knew he might explode at any moment, taking out his anger and frustration on the nearest target, and they shied away from him accordingly.

Cowards.

It wouldn't help them if he flew into a rage, as there was nowhere they could hide in camp, but Malajit was hoping that he could control himself, for once. He still had work to do, and worrying about the ambush party wouldn't get it done.

They had pitched camp between two wooded hills, drawing a measure of security from the terrain. He knew that a determined enemy could climb the far side of those hills and wriggle down to find him, but the process would be arduous, with ample room for errors that would tip the camp to their approach.

Behind the hastily erected tents, a river flowed. It gave

them free access to water and protected that flank from an infantry assault, but at the same time limited their options for retreat. Malajit had felt his men's uneasiness as they were setting up camp, but they feared him more than they feared the unseen enemy.

So far.

The hostages were huddled underneath a shelter, dead center in the camp, where he could watch them constantly if he was so inclined. The chain that linked their ankles had been staked into the ground, but even if they worked it free there was nowhere to run. They couldn't flee the camp unseen, and only heartless jungle waited for them if they managed to pull off a miracle.

Before he started worrying about the ambush party, Malajit had spent the best part of two hours puzzling over what he should do with his captives. There would be no ransom, and the prisoners were too old to interest slavers, even if Malajit could sneak them off the island and across the water to Malaysia. On the trail, they slowed him down. If government commandos found the camp, he had no reason to believe the two Americans would serve as an effective shield.

What good were they to anyone?

He longed to kill them slowly, venting his rage at their President and Congress, at the generals in Jakarta, and at anyone else who'd made his life a misery so far. It would amuse him, but it seemed a waste to Malajit. Why go through all the trouble of a kidnapping, simply to torture two old people who meant nothing to his enemies?

A thought occurred to Malajit, making him smile. Perhaps there was a satisfactory solution.

He could kill one of them and make the other watch, then release the survivor to carry the story abroad. It didn't matter how much he was reviled, but rather that the world should see his enemies for what they were—a group of heartless bureaucrats who valued their own reputations over the lives of their subjects.

How would the American press react if the preacher's widow came home alone, weeping for the cameras while she described her husband's final agony? Malajit would be demonized, of course, but he was used to that. The media was staffed with liars for the most part, but he knew some reporters who challenged policy and questioned their respective governments. Only a handful were required to probe the story, before it took on a life of its own.

It would mean running for his life, but Malajit was used to that. He'd grown up hiding from police and came of age fighting against the pigs who ruled his homeland. Running was a lifestyle long familiar to him.

It had always been the rebel's way.

Once the decision had been made, Malajit wanted to get on with it. He had no patience for procrastination, but he didn't want to rush the process, either. It was not enough to simply put the old man up before a firing squad. That was too cut-and-dried. He needed pain, and plenty of it, if he meant to tug at liberal heartstrings around the world.

Less nervous now, and smiling to himself, Garuda Malajit sat down to plan the spectacle.

"WE DON'T HAVE much time left," Amos Claridge said, speaking in a whisper to his wife.

"You can't know that," she answered, likewise whispering.

"I feel it, Merilee. You know the way I feel things, sometimes."

"You're exhausted. We both are."

Ye of little faith. He didn't voice the words. Merilee needed to believe they would escape their fate, somehow, but Claridge had begun to think in terms of martyrdom.

What else was left?

The godless heathens wouldn't let them go, and Claridge knew the government wasn't about to knuckle under with a ransom payment to a two-bit gang of terrorists halfway around the world.

"If we can leave a mark behind," he said to Merilee, "there's nothing we should fear."

"What are you saying, Amos?"

"Only that we shouldn't be afraid to die."

She was, though. He could see it in her eyes. Merilee shook her head and told him, "I can't just give up like that. It's not my way."

"You're strong, I know. Always have been. You're strong for me and strong for Jesus. But we have to face the facts sometime."

"What facts, Amos? We're still alive. If these men meant to kill us, they'd have done it at the other camp."

"I think they're running out of time, and so are we. They won't let us be rescued, if it comes to that."

The new expression on her face reminded him of hope. "You think there's someone after us?" she asked. "A rescue party? Maybe soldiers?"

"What I think is that the government will use whatever force it takes to stop this bunch, and stop them cold. We're the excuse. It's backfired on them, don't you see? They thought we were an asset, but we've turned into a liability."

"The army still might find us, Amos."

"That's what they'll be thinking, too. We didn't leave the last camp in a rush because they felt secure. The boss man didn't send a rear-guard back to watch the trail because he thinks he's safe. They're being hunted."

"Good!" she whispered. "It serves them right."

"And we die, too."

She shook her head. "I don't believe it. Just because it happened somewhere else, one time, that doesn't mean the same will happen here."

."They'll make it happen, one side or the other. Don't you see? We're meant to be a sacrifice."

She stared at him as if he'd lost his mind. The same thought had occurred to Claridge, briefly, but he'd come to the conclusion that the Lord was speaking to him, laying out His master plan.

"I'm ready, Merilee. If it's our time, Jesus will find me worthy."

"He's already found you worthy, Amos. He's not asking for your life. Not yet. And giving up's a sin. You've always told me that."

"It isn't giving up when we accept the will of God."

"If it's His will that we should die, all right, there's nothing we can do about it," Merilee replied. "But rushing it yourself is plain and simple suicide. You can't declare yourself a martyr, Amos. That is not your job!"

"I let Him guide me," he replied, "just like I always have. But I will not go weeping to the scaffold, when I have a chance to witness for the Lord."

"You're talking foolishness."

Her words felt like a slap across the face. Exhausted as he was, Claridge felt his determination slipping. If his own wife doubted him, how much could he accomplish with the little strength he still had left?

"You've never spoken to me that way in your life," he said.

"I never felt the need. But now you're giving up without a fight, and that's no compliment to Jesus. It's an insult. You weren't given life, given your calling, just to throw it away in a moment of weakness."

"And how are we supposed to fight?" he asked her, shoulders slumping. "What else would you have me do?"

"I'd have you be the man I married, Amos. As for fighting back, I'm giving it some thought."

THE REBELS HADN'T taken any pains to hide their trail. They either knew it was a waste of time, or else they'd trusted the ambush party to take down any followers who came along. In either case, Bolan was grateful for the markers left to him, and he was taking full advantage of them.

Coming up behind him, Jason Claridge stopped every thirty yards or so to scan the forest at his back. The ambush may have spooked him, but caution was good, and he seemed to be holding it together.

"How much farther, do you reckon?" he asked.

"Till we get there," Bolan said. "They could run all the way to the coast, but I doubt it. They'll look for a place to hole up."

"Where we can't root them out, I suppose."

"There's always a means. I'm betting you learned that in training."

"It isn't the same."

No, it wasn't. Where family and loved ones were concerned, a soldier lost his objectivity, and that could be a risk for all concerned. Rushing in without the proper thought could finish all of them, but so could hesitation at a crucial moment, when decisive action was required.

Finding that vital balance was the problem, when a soldier teetered on the razor's edge. A slip to either side could open wounds that never healed.

Before they started moving, Claridge checked the back-track one more time. "Somebody's coming," he told Bolan. "I can almost feel them."

"Let's use our lead, then," Bolan said, "before it slips away."

He didn't challenge the SEAL's intuition, but neither did he take the hunch as gospel truth. Instinct and gut reactions could be critical in combat, but they weren't carved in stone with a money-back guarantee.

It was probable that someone followed them, or would be following them soon. The trackers didn't have to know Bolan and Claridge existed, per se. They'd left a trail of bodies that a blind hunter could follow by the smell. It stood to reason that the army had more searchers in the field than the one small patrol he had already dodged, and sooner or later they'd pick up the trail.

That was the key. Sooner or later.

Sooner meant trouble, if they ran into a squad that knew the ground and knew its business. They'd been lucky, so far, but it couldn't last forever. Nothing ever did. Too many times at bat, and everyone struck out from time to time.

But in this game, the losers didn't get a second chance. They just got dead.

If they were being hunted, this minute, it could be a problem. But, the Executioner decided, it could also be a help, depending on the way he played his hand. A little chaos could be beneficial, when they tried to extricate the hostages.

If they could find them both alive.

He didn't want to think about Jason's reaction to the grim alternative, but Bolan had to run it through his mind as one more possible scenario. Bolan wasn't convinced that he could rein in the young SEAL, if that turned out to be the case. In fact, he wasn't even certain he should try.

There'd been no one to pull him back in Pittsfield, when he settled with the men who'd killed *his* family, but that had been a different case. His grief had chilled by then, and Bolan had approached the problem with a sniper's calculating eye. It hadn't been an act of passion, with their blood fresh on the ground.

Okay.

He'd think about it later, when he knew which way the wind was blowing. If they found the captives dead, maybe he'd help their son to scorch the earth and light a bonfire to their memory.

The rescue was his first priority, but failing that, Brognola had left disposition of the enemy to Bolan's sole discretion. And disposing of the enemy was where the Executioner excelled.

But maybe they were still alive. He couldn't count them out too soon. It was a species of betrayal, that decline of expectations. It was something close to giving up and giving in.

The two things he had never learned to do.

He meant to find the captives, one way or another.

And whatever happened next would happen in its own good time.

MAHMOUD KENDIK SMELLED THE AMBUSH site before they reached it, well before they found the first body. He wasn't in the lead this time, because his escorts had fixated on the battle sounds and because he knew this part of the terrain no better than they did. He wasn't guiding them now. He was simply along for the ride.

There weren't as many dead, as at the first shooting scene. Kendik let his companions search out the corpses, waiting for orders to view their dead faces and answer a flurry of questions. Did he know this one? Had he ever seen this face? Was he sure about that?

Five times, Kendik shook his head and answered all their questions in the negative. He didn't know these young men, had never seen them in his life until they lay before him, torn by slugs and shrapnel. Kendik wished he hadn't met them now, fearing their bad luck might infect him like a curse.

The sixth corpse, though, was different. This one, he knew. They'd spoken several times, talking product and price. Kendik had met him in the city and had traveled to the forest camp when shipments were delivered. This one had a name, and so was real.

"I know him," Kendik said.

"What was his name?" the sergeant asked.

"I only know what I was told."

"Tell me."

"Shaitan Takeri," Kendik answered. He could not betray the dead man now.

The sergeant seemed surprised, smiling. "Their second in command," he said. "I hope you're right." His mood turned thoughtful then, as he inquired, "What brings him here, I wonder? Why would Malajit send his first lieutenant on patrol?"

"I don't know, Sergeant," Kendik answered.

It was true. He knew the Sword of Freedom sometimes purchased medicine and weapons, that they always paid in cash. Kendik believed the cash was stolen—liberated, they would say—in periodic robberies, because he'd heard it said on television. No one from the group had ever told him so, and it wouldn't have mattered if they did. Money was money. Passing it from hand to hand wiped off its sins.

"You met him," the sergeant said. "More than once, was it?"

"Five times, I think. No, six." It wouldn't do for them to catch him in a lie. His bargain with Rajak Tripada had included full cooperation, and he meant to keep his word. At least, insofar as they knew.

"What did you talk about?"

"Business." He'd been through this before.

"Weapons?" the sergeant pressed.

"That's right."

"Like this?" The sergeant shook an AK-47 in his face.

"They wanted rifles. I arranged for them to meet a man who trades in such things. That is all." And he'd betrayed that man already, was responsible for his arrest and torture, likely still ongoing at Tripada's order.

"They use guns like these to kill my men," the sergeant said.

Kendik could only shrug and bite his tongue. What else would they use weapons for, except to rob and kill? It was self-evident. The sergeant wanted him to shoulder that responsibility, but Mahmoud Kendik claimed no part of it.

This wasn't his war. He supplied the highest bidders with whatever products they desired, if he could manage it. But Kendik had no part in what came next. He stayed away from politics and felt no loyalty to anyone except himself.

The sergeant leaned in close and said, "You're worse than they are. Do you know that? When they kill, at least they have a reason and the nerve to pull a trigger. You supply the killing tools, then walk away. You don't care if they're killing soldiers or old women on the street."

Kendik couldn't deny it. He shunned politics, religion, all the emotional entanglements that weakened men and made them fools. Why should he care who ran the government or who rebelled against it? Leaders, in his personal experience, were all the same. They craved power, seized it at any cost and used it to enrich themselves.

"Where will they go?" the sergeant asked.

"I've only seen the one camp, Sergeant, as you know."

"You're useless, then."

"If you prefer to leave me here…"

"I do." The sergeant drew his pistol, thumbed the hammer back and leveled it at Kendik's face.

"I may know something!" Kendik said.

"Oh, yes?"

"Another place he mentioned." He nodded at Takeri's body. "But I've never been there, never seen it."

"So? Which way?"

"South of the first camp, as we're going." Clammy sweat clung to his ribs, beneath his arms.

"You wouldn't lie to me?" The sergeant sneered.

"No, sir."

"Let's find out, shall we? Take the lead."

MERILEE CLARIDGE hesitated in the midst of prayer and realized that she had nothing more to say. She had already asked the Lord for strength and for deliverance. No answer was forthcoming, and it struck her that she was alone.

It hadn't been that way while Amos persevered and had the will to hope, but he had given up on everything. His faith, their life together, life itself. She'd never seen this martyr complex manifest itself before, but it had pushed her to the stark edge of despair.

Almost.

Unlike her husband, she would not give up. The truth was, Merilee Claridge had never learned how to surrender. She wasn't a quitter. Never had been, and never would be.

Submission was one thing—to Jesus, to Amos in marriage—but that was an act of love and respect. Throwing her life away would be the very opposite, an insult to her loved ones and the God who had created her.

She thought of Jason as she'd seen him last, in his dress uniform, and wondered how he was. Worried, of course, and frightened for his parents. She could only hope that the routines of navy life distracted him somewhat, filling the time that otherwise would be a waking nightmare for him. He was strong, no doubt about it, but he'd never faced a test like this. She hoped that he would pass it and move on, whatever happened next. If she and Amos were killed—

Don't think that way! You're tempting God.

Or, maybe not.

Her faith caused Merilee to think that all things happened for a reason, as ordained by their Father in Heaven. She understood that righteous souls were tested by the Devil, with

God's blessing, to insure that they were pure, but she'd never reckoned God to be capricious.

Never once, until they'd been abducted by the men who held them prisoner.

It seemed to Merilee that she and Amos had already proved themselves, by giving up their life and home in the United States to rescue heathens from the everlasting fire. They had endured hardship, hunger, poverty—all for the sake of saving souls. They weren't like Job, who'd prospered and grown wealthy to the point that God believed he needed testing, to find out if he was faithful.

They'd done nothing wrong, that she could see.

Why were they being punished, then?

There was another way to look at it, of course. Some of the saints were caged, tortured and executed for their faith. Jesus himself had gone that route and offered every man redemption through His blood. If she pursued that line of thought, perhaps their suffering made sense.

And yet, she wasn't sure.

That doubt was a subversive impulse. It betrayed her, but she couldn't shake it. Now that Death stood facing her, she had to wonder if her life had been well spent, or whether it had been a waste. If she'd been wrong from the beginning, from her childhood, it would mean she'd squandered all those years serving a false god who was powerless to aid her in a time of trial.

That's Satan talking. Get thee behind me, Devil!

But she couldn't dam the flow of unbidden, unwelcome thoughts that swirled inside her head. Beside her, Amos sat with his legs crossed, hands limp in his lap, unconsciously mimicking a yoga posture. Merilee couldn't tell if he was praying, or if he had slipped into some kind of daze. His lips weren't moving, as they often did when he prayed silently. Thin as he was, she had to double-check to see if he was breathing.

Yes.

While life remained, there might be hope.

But who could save them now? If divine intervention was out of the question, what power could pluck them from captivity in such a remote wilderness? Who even cared enough to try?

She felt the dark imp of despair perched on her shoulder, whispering its message of defeat.

Softly and hopelessly, she wept.

RAJAK TRIPADA READ the message that his aide brought from the communications room, fresh off the printer after it had been relayed by two-way radio. His hunters in the field had found more bodies, evidence of yet another skirmish between rebels and some unknown opposition force. They were proceeding southward, following Mahmoud Kendik to seek a place one of his contacts in the Sword of Freedom had described. A place their guide had never seen.

It was a risk, potentially a waste of precious time, but as he read the note again, Tripada had a premonition of success. This time, he thought, they had a chance to crush the traitors, to eliminate them once and for all.

It was an opportunity he couldn't miss.

The man who killed Garuda Malajit or brought him back for public trial would be a hero. They would love him in Jakarta—where, of course, he was already held in high esteem. This would be different, though, an altogether perfect feather in his cap.

The only drawback was that he could not claim credit for the deed unless he joined his soldiers in the field. If he hung back and waited for the news that Malajit was dead or caged, some of the men who now supported him might wonder if their trust had been misplaced. They might decide to elevate another. And for someone new to rise, it meant that someone else must fall.

"Go back," Tripada told his aide, "and tell them that I plan to join them."

"Sir?" The young lieutenant seemed confused.

"You heard me. I am joining the patrol and will be with them, in command, when they confront the enemy."

"Yes, sir."

As the lieutenant turned to go, Tripada stopped him. "Wait. How many special forces troops can be collected in an hour?"

"From the barracks, sir, perhaps thirty."

Tripada frowned. It wasn't much, but it would have to do. "After you send that message—no, before you send it—place them on alert. I want two helicopters ready to take off within the hour. Get coordinates from the patrol and give them to the pilots."

"Yes, sir."

This time, when the lieutenant stalled, Tripada waved him toward the door. "Dismissed."

When he was left alone, Tripada ran a mental checklist of his preparations for the journey. He would change into fatigues and draw gear from the quartermaster, choose a weapon from the armory and think of some brief comment for the men who'd follow him. They wouldn't ask for explanations, and he owed them none, but something in the nature of a pep talk would not be amiss.

He could remind them of their duty to the nation and its people, brief them on the gravity of their endeavor. If they triumphed and destroyed the enemy, they would be well rewarded. Those who fell in battle would be honored by the government, their families—

On second thought, he would delete that last bit. It was foolish to remind a group of soldiers facing battle that they might be dead within the next few hours. If they didn't realize it, going in, they had to be idiots.

Stay positive. Be optimistic.

Tripada imagined his return from combat and the welcome he'd receive for shattering the Sword of Freedom. Promotion, decoration, possibly a transfer to Jakarta. He could see it all within his grasp.

Now, all he had to do was make it happen.

Flying in to join the strike team was the easy part. Command was his by right and could not be refused. Having secured the unit, though, he'd also have to lead it, or allow the guide to lead them in a way that made Tripada seem decisive. More than simply competent.

He'd been in combat only once, and that had been nine years ago, but some things weren't forgotten once they had been learned. Skills might grow rusty, but he'd kept himself in shape and qualified with small arms, setting an example for his men.

Only the jungle troubled him, the unfamiliar ground they would be penetrating, searching for their hidden enemies. Garuda Malajit knew the terrain and would do everything within his power to destroy them, or to at least avoid capture.

The outcome wasn't settled yet, could not be guaranteed. Tripada wished that he could take a hundred men, instead of thirty, but he would make do with what he had.

And he would win. Failure was unacceptable.

If they were not victorious, Tripada vowed, none of his people would return alive.

12

How much longer?

Jason Claridge hadn't asked again, but Bolan was prepared to ask the question of himself. He was following the trail his adversaries left, playing connect-the-dots and leaving bodies in his wake, but he couldn't have said they were closer to finding the captives today than they were yesterday.

Slogging through rain that plastered down his hair and soaked him to the skin, Bolan could only wonder if his enemies would stop to wait it out, camp for the night, or if they'd keep marching toward some destination yet unknown to him. If they held their present course, they should run out of island in another hundred miles or so, but there was nothing to prevent them veering off in one direction or another, circling endlessly through jungles older than the human race.

Bolan's fierce determination would insure that they wouldn't slip away.

The intermittent rain made tracking difficult. If he'd been trailing a lone adversary, even two or three, Bolan guessed they could've given him the slip by now. Step off the trail, get lost to one side or the other, and he could've passed them by without a clue. It was a lucky break, then, that the trail he followed had been trampled down by several dozen men.

Lucky.

Until Bolan overtook them on their own turf, spoiling for a fight, and found his two-man team outnumbered by twenty or thirty to one.

He'd done all right so far, with Claridge, but they hadn't faced a test with overwhelming odds. An ambush or a running skirmish in the woods was one thing. A pitched battle was very different, and many times more dangerous. Toss in a rescue plan for hostages, caged who knew where, and he had a recipe for potential disaster.

It wasn't strictly accurate to say he had a rescue plan, of course. All Bolan had in mind, so far, was the ideal scenario: a simple in-and-out, no sentries interrupting them, no one the wiser as they freed the prisoners and fled without a trace. In the ideal scenario there was no firefight, no more killing. Granted, it went easy on the rebels, leaving them to fight another day, but with the hostages in hand, the Sword of Freedom would be someone else's problem.

Bolan seldom took the path of least resistance, but he looked for simple shortcuts when civilians were involved. Bystanders, hostages, employees—if they weren't colluding with the enemy and threatening his life or mission, Bolan did his best to see that they weren't harmed.

And sometimes he failed.

In this case, if he found the hostages alive, they would be under guard. In essence, every rebel in the party was a jailer, theoretically committed to preventing an escape or rescue. Bolan wasn't sure how many men and weapons that included, but they had enough to do the job.

If they were good enough.

The scouts and stragglers he had encountered to that point struck him as average. One common failing of guerrilla forces was a lack of thorough training, whether from the inexperience of their commanders, indolence among the troops, or shortage of supplies. They might not have enough ammo for steady target practice. Maybe some of them were tired of fighting, slowly letting down their guard. Since Bolan didn't know his enemies, he couldn't judge their weaknesses definitively. But from what he'd seen, the Sword of Freedom had its share of flaws.

All Bolan had to do was spot those failings, turn them to his own advantage, free the hostages and take them safely back to Subic Bay.

Simple. In theory, anyway.

The rub came when a soldier started putting theory into practice on a real-life battlefield and saw it shot to hell in the first two minutes of engagement. From that point onward, plans went out the window and it became a raw fight for survival. If that happened, the couple he hoped to extract would be caught in the middle with nowhere to hide.

Each step took Bolan closer to the moment of that showdown, where theory and reality collided in the jungle. He wished they were already done and on the other side of it, but wishing was for dreamers. Bolan was a realist, and there were damned few happy endings in his nightmare world.

If Jason Claridge pulled his weight and didn't lose it at the first glimpse of his parents, they might succeed. If Claridge couldn't keep himself on a short leash, their chances of survival were reduced. The SEAL knew that, had processed the fact intellectually, but Bolan still feared that his emotions would betray him in the crunch.

Bolan would cope with that problem if and when he faced it. Meanwhile, he was taking Claridge as he took the jungle manhunt.

One step at a time.

MAHMOUD KENDIK HATED the rain. It drenched him, thrust cold fingers inside his collar, filled his boots and generally made life miserable. He was literally sick of marching, with a headache that pulsed in time to his steps, while his stomach churned alarmingly.

Kendik imagined some obscure bacteria or virus racing through his bloodstream, withering his organs one by one. The image made his headache worse, and there was no relief in sight. Between his soggy boots and trousers, Kendik's feet felt like a pair of leaden weights.

There was good news and bad news.

Good news first: The rain had slowed their march, thus buying extra time before they overtook their quarry and were forced into a deadly fight. Kendik had hoped they might get lost, but his escorts were special forces, trained in jungle navigation and a host of other arcane skills. They wouldn't quit unless headquarters countermanded their instructions and recalled them from the quest.

Bad news: Rajak Tripada would be joining them with reinforcements, sometime in the next half hour. It had been arranged by radio, while they were at the ambush site. The strike team would be coming in by helicopter, homing on coordinates provided by the ground squad's leader. Once they landed, the enhanced force would resume pursuit of their intended prey with all deliberate speed.

Kendik had no love for Rajak Tripada, but he thought this time the dour security chief might have done him a favor. When they met the helicopters, there would be a measure of confusion on the ground. Enough, perhaps, for him to slip away unseen and flee into the forest, if his escorts dropped their guard.

Kendik realized it was a faint hope, but still better than none.

More bad news: By the time he got his chance to run—if there was any chance at all—Kendik would be several miles farther from civilization, alone in the jungle. Alone in the dark.

That troubled him, but not as much as the thought of being caught in a firefight, pinned in a bloody cross fire with no weapon and no hope seeing another sunrise.

Alone, even alone and lost, he might just have a chance. There were no tigers or other large predators on Borneo to stalk him in the dark. Snakes and small jungle cats were his only risk, as far as wildlife was concerned, and Kendik had no fear of them. Tramping through the jungle night, a sprained or broken leg was both more likely and more dangerous. If he was injured accidentally, so far from human aid, it would mean nearly certain death.

Two points of danger, then. The first, escaping from his escorts without being shot. The second, everything that followed his escape.

Kendik didn't believe the soldiers would pursue him very far, if he should have a chance to run. They had no further use for him, and with Tripada pressing them to reach their goal, fulfill their mission, there would be no time to waste. Tripada might remember him, however, when he got back to the city.

If the two of them returned alive from their adventure in the dark.

One problem at a time. He had a better chance on city streets than in the wilderness, but it would be a long, hard slog to reach that sanctuary.

It would be the challenge of his life.

The rain picked up, drumming against his floppy bush hat, soaking through to chill his scalp. Marching without lights, without speaking, Kendik couldn't tell if they were still on course or walking in a circle without end. The point man held their lives in the same hand that gripped his compass—but did he, in fact, know where they were?

I should've brought a compass, Kendik thought, but it was foolishness. He hadn't been allowed to choose equipment when they dressed him for the mission. He was lucky to have clothes that fit.

And he'd never learned to use a compass, anyway.

Just wait. You'll know the moment when it comes.

He hoped so. Prayed that it was true.

For Mahmoud Kendik sensed that he was running out of time.

THE PRISONERS WERE brought before Garuda Malajit by four armed escorts, flanking them as if they had the strength to overpower fighting men, seize weapons and fight their way out of the camp. It was a waste of manpower, but Malajit believed in ceremony when it counted.

He was seated on a tree stump when they joined him, rough bark chafing at him through the wet fabric of his fatigue pants. Malajit felt anything but lordly, squatting on his awkward throne, but it was all that he could think of. Lighting fires posed too much risk, even if they could find enough dry wood to set one burning.

Seated on the stump and looking up at his two prisoners, Malajit suddenly felt diminished. He lurched to his feet and clasped hands behind his back, standing at ease in front of them.

Their lives were his.

They knew it.

He could see it in their eyes.

Malajit cleared his throat and said, "Your government refuses every offer to release you safely. They prefer to pose for photographs and threaten freedom fighters they can never touch, much less destroy. Such arrogance has hampered my attempts to set you free."

The captives watched him, level-eyed. They did not speak.

"Your choice to visit Borneo was not a wise one," he went on. "I don't know whether you are spies for the United States, or simply trespassers who feel you have the right to force your gods and fables onto others."

"We have only one God, sir," the man replied.

"Silence!" The sudden rage felt good. It kept him warm against the rain. "You have nothing to say here. No more pleas for souls or money. You are finished in this country. Finished everywhere."

They stared at him in stony silence. Darkness shrouded them. The rain fell on them like a judgment from above.

"You stand accused of meddling in the lives of free and sovereign people, causing some to leave their native culture in pursuit of your subversive creeds. Additionally, you are charged with being agents of the West and of the traitors in Jakarta, who enslave our people and deny their right of self-determination. You are spies and saboteurs. How do you plead?"

Silence.

Malajit felt his anger simmering. "Answer!"

"You've told us not to speak," the man reminded him.

"When asked a question," Malajit responded stiffly, "you will answer. Is that understood?"

"Of course."

"All right. How do you plead?"

"I plead for reason in the face of madness," said the minister. "And failing that, I pray for strength to deal with Satan and his minions."

"What?"

"My feet are planted on the Rock of Ages. While the power of the Lord is with me, I will fear no evil. His rod and staff shall—"

Malajit stepped forward, snarling as he swung a fist into the man's face. The preacher staggered, seemed on the verge of falling, but somehow found his balance and remained upright.

"Our Father—"

Malajit kicked sharply at the preacher's knee. The prayer ended abruptly with a squeal of pain, as the man collapsed. At once, his wife knelt over him, prepared to shield his body with her own.

"You've said enough," Malajit told his stricken prisoner. "I find you guilty of all charges, as described. The only fitting punishment is death."

The woman turned and gaped at him, as if unable to accept his words. "You mean to murder us?" she asked.

"He will be executed," Malajit replied, correcting her. "I grant you mercy, though you're certainly as guilty as he is. Your penalty is exile from this island under pain of death if you return. You will go back to the United States and tell what you have seen. Explain how spies and interlopers meet their end beneath the Sword of Freedom."

"I won't leave him," she said defiantly.

Malajit shrugged. "The choice is yours. When we are finished with him, you may carry what is left out of the jungle— if you can."

"What kind of animal are you?"

"I am a free man and a patriot. You've come to *my* country. I didn't come to yours. This is the price you pay for meddling where you don't belong."

"Our Lord commands us to preach his gospel in every corner of the Earth, to every tribe and nation."

"Yes? I see. Where is he, then?" Malajit waited, frowning. "Why does he not rescue you, or strike me dead?"

"He will, in time," she said.

"In time, perhaps," said Malajit. "But not in time for you. The execution will proceed at sunrise. You will watch, and learn."

A FEW YEARS EARLIER, it would've been impossible for Rajak Tripada to find his soldiers in the forest without lighting fires or using signal flares, and thus alerting every enemy within a five-mile radius. But thanks to the proliferation of the latest GPS technology, his pilots could deposit reinforcements on the spot, with no significant margin of error.

High-tech toys were wonderful things, Tripada reflected, but the view from his seat in the UH-60 Black Hawk helicopter revealed a primordial world down below. Beneath the moon-dappled canopy of forest, lost in the Stygian shadows, predators and prey were locked in the same death struggle they had pursued from time immemorial. It would've been no great surprise to see a dinosaur down there, less still a tribe of primitives unsullied by the Midas touch of so-called civilization.

It was a different world, and he would soon be down there in the dark, with less than fifty men around him, hunting traitors in the forest. When the smoke cleared, only then could he distinguish between victors and the vanquished.

If he lived that long.

Tripada rarely went into the field himself, and this adventure was unprecedented. It could make or break him back at headquarters. If he retrieved the two Americans, he'd be a hero. Better yet, if he could crush the Sword of Freedom, no one in Jakarta would care anything about what happened to the Yanks.

They were intruders, anyway. Two arrogant zealots who wandered the planet, inflicting their views on the rest of the world.

No great loss.

He heard the pilots jabbering to someone on the radio, then one of them leaned back and said, "Five minutes to the drop zone, sir."

Tripada nodded, checking his gear one last time. A landing would've been too hazardous at night, among the giant trees, so they'd be dropping to the ground on static lines.

They wouldn't plummet to the earth like bungee jumpers, and there'd be no giddy rebound to the heavens—if they did it properly. A smooth descent was all Tripada asked, to plant his feet once more on solid ground.

And then the last phase of the hunt could finally begin.

He wore a pistol and a canteen on his belt, with extra ammunition magazines and a stout knife for hacking brush. Across his lap, its sling wrapped carefully around one arm, an M-16 assault rifle provided extra firepower. The bandolier across his chest was heavy, its canvas strap already chafing his shoulder, but Tripada could live with it. And he might die without it.

The strike team carried only pocket rations, since they had no intention of waging a drawn-out campaign. From the rendezvous point, they would march at top speed in pursuit of the targets his ground team had tracked through the long afternoon. His enemies could not march day and night. They would make camp soon, if they hadn't done so already, and he would surprise them as they slept or sat around a small fire, swapping lies.

Tonight, he would be done with it and on to better things.

A shift in the helicopter's vibration told him they were hovering, instead of moving forward. Tripada peered through the open cargo bay, fighting a momentary rush of vertigo, and saw the winking eyes of flashlight beams below. His men were down there, signaling the choppers, marking out the drop zone with their lights.

"It's time to go, sir," the pilot called from his cockpit seat. He flashed a thumbs-up, which Tripada pointedly ignored.

He had been briefed on the procedure prior to takeoff, and Tripada knew exactly what he had to do. The first step was a killer, exiting the aircraft over yawning darkness, but he did it, and the static line supported him with only minimal discomfort. There was a dead-man's clip for him to squeeze with his left hand and play out line, controlling the rate of his drop. If his hand slipped, there would be no plunging into the abyss. The line would hold him fast.

Around him, members of the special forces team were out and halfway to the ground. Their speed encouraged him to hurry, working on his form in case one of the flashlight beams should pick him out. There was a thrill of sorts, like riding in a high-speed elevator from the penthouse to the basement, without stopping in between.

A moment later, he was on the ground and working on the buckles of his harness. When the empty rigging had been snatched away, the helicopters wheeling out of sight and beating through the night air back to their secure berths at the military base, Tripada looked around and found the soldiers watching him. Their painted faces were expectant, waiting.

"You all know why we're here," he said. "Tonight, it ends. If we do not destroy the traitors, we do not return alive."

"And the Americans, sir?" a voice behind him asked.

"We'll bring them out, if possible. If not…" He shrugged and said, "Fortunes of war. Who knows the way?"

"We have the trail, sir."

"Good. We're wasting time."

NEAR MIDNIGHT, Jason Claridge saw the man walking in front of him stop dead, as if he'd walked into a solid wall. Claridge did likewise, picking up the danger signal without spoken words.

He watched and listened, straining for some hint of what had spooked Cooper. Even though the rain had backed off to a nagging drizzle, water still fell from the trees around him, pattering on impact, muffling any other sounds that may have raised alarm flags with his stolid comrade. Staring into darkness, he saw nothing that suggested movement to the front, or on their flanks.

If only he had some idea—

He heard it then, almost completely smothered by the sounds of dripping water. Voices. Up ahead, perhaps no farther than a hundred yards, at least two human beings were engaged in conversation. From the sound of it, albeit muffled by the night and distance, they were not expecting company. He wondered if the enemy would be that careless, and it came to him that there were doubtless natives in the forest, maybe some along his line of march.

And if the people talking up ahead weren't targets, they were obstacles. He and Cooper would have to work around them, at the risk of setting off alarms if they were spotted, maybe triggering some warning to the rebels they pursued.

We've got no friends out here, he thought, resting his index finger lightly on the carbine's trigger.

Just in case.

Cooper eased forward and motioned for Claridge to follow. The young SEAL took it slow and easy, wincing every time his boots squelched in the mud. That sound had been a kind of static background noise before, but now he reckoned it was loud enough to wake the dead.

More voices came to Claridge as they closed the gap. He couldn't tell how many men were speaking, much less translate what they said. It was a kind of murmur, yet it told him they were closing in on something more than two stray hunters swapping tall tales in the dark.

Though they were barely creeping now, their progress seemed too swift, too loud. Claridge was sure that any second one of the unseen babblers would perk up his ears and warn the others of intruders close at hand. Grappling with his fatigue and nerves, Claridge stepped cautiously, as if he were proceeding through a mine field.

Moments later, Cooper paused again, and this time signaled Claridge to come forward. Moving to join him, Claridge found that he was walking in a crouch that made the muscles in his legs ache, staying low by instinct rather than volition. With an effort, Claridge brought himself erect and took his place on Cooper's right.

The camp was still some fifty yards away, but he could make out firelight now, faint as it was, with shadow figures moving back and forth against the lighter backdrop. They were too far out for spotting faces, uniforms, insignia, but he could see the men were armed.

"It's them," he whispered.

"Probably."

"Okay. What now?"

"We check out the perimeter," Bolan replied, his answer barely audible. "They chose this campsite for a reason. If it gives them an edge, we need to know that, going in."

"You want the left or right?" asked Claridge.

"Right's good."

"Should we synchronize?"

Bolan considered it, then shook his head. "No point. We can't coordinate a move until we scope the turf. See how the land lies, then come back and we can work it out."

More fleeting time, but Claridge knew his companion was right. He might find nothing to obstruct him on the right, while Cooper was ass-deep in alligators on the left. Or should he make that crocodiles?

Whatever.

Even though he longed to go in shooting, raze the camp and drag his parents out of there, they still had some preliminary work to do. Scouting the target, counting heads and guns if possible, and maybe—this one was a long shot, he admitted to himself—collecting some intelligence on where his parents were.

If they were here at all.

He couldn't make himself believe they'd found the wrong

camp after all their effort, somehow stumbled on a different band of gunmen in the jungle. No. The odds against such a coincidence were so extreme that Claridge judged it practically impossible.

But that still didn't mean he'd find his parents in the camp. They could've been discarded on the trail, bypassed in rainy darkness while he followed their abductors.

They might already be dead, fresh meat for scavengers, and he might never find them.

Never.

And if that turned out to be the case, Claridge promised himself, there would be hell to pay.

BOLAN STAYED as close to camp as possible while scouting the perimeter. There wasn't much to see at first, by the light of one small fire, but he stayed with it, working on a head count, noting any weapons that were visible, plotting the rough arrangement of tents in his mind. It seemed to be haphazard, which could work against them in a panic, but it also worked against the rebels if they didn't have the layout memorized.

He'd traveled fifty yards or so before the ground began to rise. Bolan was conscious of the change at once, noting the extra effort required for each step as he started to climb. High ground would normally have pleased him, if it was a sniping situation, but he didn't plan any long-distance work tonight. Still, if he watched his step and didn't make unnecessary noise, climbing the hill would grant him an improved perspective of the rebel camp.

He took his time, not rushing it. No hasty thrashing noises to alert the enemy below. Reconnaissance wasn't about contact. It was about preparing for contact, and that was best done quietly, without attention from the other side.

The hill was fairly steep, something like sixty-five de-

grees. Bolan was thankful for the mud now, even though it
made him slip and clutch at trees or vines to keep from skid-
ding down the slope. It also guaranteed that no misstep would
send a noisy shower of dirt and stones cascading down the
hill to warn his enemies that they were being watched.

Five minutes in, he found a vantage point that suited him
and braced himself against a tree to keep from sliding while
he scanned the camp below. From there, he saw the river he'd
been hearing as he climbed, a backdrop that prevented any
swift retreat from camp, but which also required any attack-
ers from that quarter to make an amphibious landing. Bolan
guessed there would be sentries on the river bank, unless the
man in charge down there was totally inept.

And then he saw the hostages.

Bolan had missed them on the first pass for the simple reason that they had been planted in the middle of the camp, beneath a shelter half that screened them from a watcher to the
south. The fire had been between him and their small half-
tent, and they were cloaked in shadow. Bolan only saw them
now because one of the prisoners shifted position, allowing
a moonbeam to glint on the chain that secured him or her.

Chained in the middle of the camp, surrounded by the
enemy. It could've been worse, Bolan thought. They could've
been perched on the edge of a cliff, for example, or squeezed
into a tunnel where he couldn't see them at all. Hell, they
could've been caged on the moon.

It would be tough, but maybe not impossible.

He spent another moment there, revised his head count up-
ward to the high side of three dozen guns, and reckoned it
would be no picnic coming in through their front door. That
was the only option left to Bolan, though, unless Claridge
could find a soft spot on the eastern side.

Descending, Bolan made good use of gravity and let it pull
him down the hillside, trusting the same handholds he had

used while climbing to head off an uncontrolled slide. It was easier going down, and much quicker. He reached level ground in half the time it had taken him to climb the hillside—and he froze there, as the sound of breaking wind announced the presence of an enemy.

Napoleon once said an army marched on its stomach. But the off-key music of digestion was sometimes enough to get a soldier killed.

The lookout played another sour note, and Bolan had him. One wasn't enough to get the fix, but on the second Bolan started moving, easing his knife from its sheath. This kill needed to be as silent as the Executioner could make it, and the muffled Glock would be too loud. A blade should be just right, unless he gave the sentry time to squeal or fire a warning shot.

It almost seemed to Bolan that he was advancing in slow motion, but he closed the gap by measured strides, stalking the man who had emerged from cover to become a silhouette before him. Bolan's target was facing south toward the grueling line of march, so the soldier worked around behind him, with the camp at his own back.

Another thirty feet would do it, but he had to take his time. At twenty, Bolan froze again and waited for the guy to scratch himself. All class. Fifteen was close enough for him to rush the sentry, but he didn't want to risk the noise. At ten, he drew a breath and held it, eyes locked on the dead man standing. Five was close enough to smell his target, who would never be mistaken for a rose.

The sentry may have known that he was dying, but he couldn't stop it. Bolan clamped a hand across his quarry's mouth and twisted sharply to the left, while stamping down with his right foot behind the guy's right knee. Dropping, the lookout met the blade on its ascent, the cold steel burrowing beneath his jaw, slicing the jugular and the carotid artery en route to finding the junction of his spine and skull. One brutal thrust and it was done.

Bolan made no attempt to hide the body. He was on his way to meet with Jason Claridge, and if nothing kept the SEAL from coming back, they should be on the move within minutes. If the rebels had a shift change coming up before that happened, he would simply have to live with it.

Or die with it.

Whichever way it went, one thing was carved in stone. There'd be more blood before the sun came up, and a number of those standing underneath the stars would never see it rise.

13

Merilee Claridge's captors had taken her wristwatch the first night they camped, and she'd been guessing the time ever since. It hadn't mattered for the past few days, but it was crucial now. She had to know when sunrise would come.

And how much longer Amos had to live.

She had been planning methods of escape while he ignored her, praying silently, eyes tightly shut. More accurately, she had fantasized escaping from the camp, since there was no way she could break the chain that tethered them, much less slip past their enemies to reach the forest.

And even if they could do all of that, where would they go?

Hopeless.

She recognized despair, and though it galled her, she could not deny the feeling. Merilee could've tried praying with Amos, but where had supplication gotten them so far? What good had it ever done, for that matter?

Where was God when she needed Him?

The Lord helped those who helped themselves.

But if that was the case, why did He cast His faithful servants into situations where they could do nothing but sit back and wait for death?

Was that the final message? Was it all a childish exercise in futility?

"Amos." She nudged him sharply with her elbow, but he kept his eyes closed, pale lips moving silently in prayer. "Amos! You need to pay attention now. We have to do something. We can't just sit here, waiting."

He turned to face her then. To Merilee, it seemed that his eyes took a moment to focus, as if he'd been staring across some boundless panoramic view and she had interrupted him.

"There's nothing to be done," he said. "God's will cannot be challenged."

"Amos, listen to me now. For once, hear me." She gripped his forearm, fingers digging deep. "We don't know that this is God's will. There's been no sign of that at all. You're giving up, and that's a sin against the Lord."

His smile shocked her. "What can I do? The trial is nearly over. You will take the message to the faithful."

"Message? What message, Amos? Have you lost your mind?"

The smile had gone from shocking to infuriating.

"Merilee," he said with saintly patience, as if speaking to someone simpleminded, "the message hasn't changed. We all abide in faith and meet whatever end our Father has in store for us. His will be done."

Merilee knew that she had lost him, and her sense of helplessness deepened. She was convinced his mind had snapped at last. Now she would have to think and plan for both of them, treating her husband as a senile invalid.

What difference does it make? she asked herself. We're trapped, regardless.

Maybe he was better off, at that, without a true grasp of their desperate situation. Maybe it would help him in the final moments of his life.

But who would give her strength to watch him slaughtered, and to live on afterward?

"Amos…"

Merilee had not formed a coherent thought, but anything she'd hoped to say was swept immediately from her mind as gunfire rocked the camp, stilling the conversations of her captors. Amos turned in the direction of the sound, frowning, as if another interruption might be more than he could tolerate.

"I'm praying here!" he shouted at the wall of darkened trees beyond the firelight. "Show the Lord Almighty some goddamned respect!"

She might have laughed, but chaos had erupted in the camp. There was more shooting now, although she couldn't track the noise to a specific source. It seemed to come from everywhere at once. Their captors ran in all directions, shouting in their native tongue.

"It's blasphemy!" Amos cried. "Damned impertinence!"

Slipping an arm around his shoulders, Merilee whispered, "Or maybe it's deliverance."

A SOFT PROBE of the rebel camp was hopeless. Even if they'd waited for the fire to die and all their enemies to fall asleep, Bolan had known there'd be no way to free the prisoners and exit from the killing ground without a fight. And when collision was inevitable, he subscribed to certain basic rules.

Hit first.

Hit hard.

Hit often.

When all else fails, raise hell.

If they couldn't sneak into the camp, they'd blast their way in, trusting darkness, drowsiness and panic to confuse their enemies at first. From that point on, they would need nerve, firepower and a fair amount of luck to make it out alive.

Chaos, by definition, had no pattern. After sorting out their angles of attack, Bolan and Claridge hit their stations, sixty yards apart, and crept as closely as they could to the perimeter. Before their time ran out, Bolan had dropped another sentry, clubbing this one from behind with his rifle and standing on his throat to finish it.

He made it to his mark on time and waited, hoping Claridge wasn't hung up on the way. Hoping he wouldn't blow it out of haste or rage.

Close up, the camp looked relatively normal. If it hadn't been for the assault weapons and ragtag uniforms, it could've been mistaken for a logging camp or a wilderness retreat. With the AKs and other hardware, though, it was a lethal hornet's nest.

Bolan lined up his nearest targets, two men lounging on the ground outside a tent, twenty feet away. They didn't see Death crouching in the darkness, didn't have a clue that they were almost out of time.

After the first shots had been fired, they had a relatively simple plan. Blast through the camp, converging on the hostages and dropping anyone who moved in that direction. Free them somehow, gunning through the chain, or whatever it took, and exit toward the river. If and when they reached its shore, they would turn westward, put the camp behind them, run like hell.

If they were still alive and mobile, right.

His first short burst of 5.56 mm tumblers strafed the lounging rebels, flattened them beside their canvas shelter. Up and running, Bolan found another target even as he heard the almost-echo of his own fire, coming from the barrel of a CAR-15.

Three down, then four, and suddenly the camp was filled with muzzle-flashes. Anybody who could reach a gun was firing, most of them without a clear-cut target. A grenade exploded off to Bolan's left, and when the shock wave passed him, screams were mingled with the automatic weapons fire.

Some of the rebels had been sleeping when it started.

Bolan caught them crawling out of tents, dragging rifles behind them, bleary-eyed, confused and frightened. One of them was right in front of him, a young man Jason's age, turning his face to meet the apparition bearing down on him. A point-blank shot between the eyes put him to sleep for good.

Time's wasting.

Bolan ducked and rolled as two guerrillas came up firing, streams of bullets from their rifles sizzling through the air above his head. He shot one of them through the hip, dropped him and pivoted to gut the other with a blazing figure eight that punched him over on his back.

The wounded rebel couldn't stand, but he was still a threat. He hadn't dropped his weapon, and despite his agony, he was fixated on destroying his opponent. Another burst from fifteen feet opened his chest and left him twitching in the dirt.

Another frag grenade went off, smoke swirling at the epicenter of the blast while shrapnel buzzed across the camp. Jason's?

There was no time to think about it as the Executioner regained his feet and started running in a zigzag pattern toward the prisoners.

It would be all for nothing if he found them dead.

But it would not be done.

THE LEADER of the Sword of Freedom was dozing when the first shots sounded in camp. Malajit bolted upright in his tent and lost his balance from the sudden rush of blood to his head. Reeling, he tripped on his own rumpled blanket and fell painfully on his backside.

The fall saved his life, as a rifle slug ripped through the tent, in and out, passing two inches above his head. If he had been standing, the shot would've gutted him and maybe clipped his spine. Sure death, under the circumstances, either swift or slow.

Perhaps it was a sign.

Malajit found his rifle, cocked it and crawled out of the tent, staying low all the way. The shock wave from a hand grenade explosion nearly pushed him back inside, spraying his face with gritty mud, but he was unscathed by its shrapnel.

Almost certainly a sign.

His soldiers were running around in a panic, many of them firing aimlessly into the jungle that surrounded them. Shouting for order in the camp, Malajit moved among them, heedless of the danger to himself.

He felt invulnerable. Blessed.

Grabbing a sleeve here, a lapel there, slapping the faces of those who resisted, he gradually organized a rifle squad out of the chaos while bullets filled the air around him. Another grenade exploded, its breath like a draft from Hell, but he barely felt the steel shards plucking at his uniform.

"Stand fast!" he shouted. "Form a skirmish line! Fall in!"

They obeyed him reluctantly, flinching at each new burst of automatic fire, but they obeyed. In desperate times, sheer force of personality could sometimes make the difference between defeat and victory, survival or annihilation.

"We have two missions," Malajit explained. "First, to secure the prisoners, and at the same time rally the remainder of our comrades to defend the camp, if they don't shoot one another first."

A bullet sizzled past his face, but Malajit ignored it. He was standing on the verge of something great, some breakthrough that would finally assure him of his place in history.

Turning toward the center of the camp, where he had chained the hostages, Malajit clutched his AK-47 in a death grip as he shouted, "Follow me!"

The camp vaguely reminded Malajit of Hell, as he'd seen it portrayed long years ago, in children's Bible storybooks.

Damaged bodies writhed and twitched around his feet, a couple of the tents were burning, and the reek of cordite filled his nostrils. Maybe not the same as brimstone, but the next best thing.

But if the battleground was Hell, then what did that make him? Was he the Devil, or a savior of his people long oppressed? And did it really matter, either way?

As best as he could remember the religious lessons of his childhood, Satan held dominion over Earth. It was the only venue Malajit had ever known. If he was choosing sides, why not select the winner?

Moving toward the shelter where the prisoners were kept, he used brute force to gather men along the way. One tried to break away from Malajit and got a bullet for his trouble, thus persuading his companions to be quick as they fell into line. Bullets still flew among them, striking down a rebel here and there, but Malajit ignored them.

For the balance of this night, at least, he felt that he could do no wrong.

The world was his to claim. He simply had to grab it by the throat and hold on for dear life.

RAJAK TRIPADA HEARD fresh sounds of combat in the middle distance, closer than he might have hoped. Another battle in the night, and from the echoes he was certain there were more than half a dozen guns involved.

"Hurry!" he shouted at the troops around him. "They will not escape again."

The sergeant hesitated to obey. "With all respect, sir," he suggested, "there are risks involved in running through the jungle in the middle of the night."

"A calculated risk that you've been paid to face," Tripada snapped. "Now, lead these men at double time, or I'll find someone else who can!"

"Yes, sir!" The sergeant spun away, rigid, and bawled at his commandos, "Double-time! On me!"

They set off jogging through the dark, still slower than a sprint, but nearly twice the pace they'd been maintaining for the past few hours. Tripada believed himself fit for a man of his age, but he soon felt the burn in his calves and thighs, the jolting discomfort to his lower back that came from speeding over rugged ground. A slip at this speed could snap ankle bones or pitch him off to one side of the narrow trail, beyond the line of march.

Would any of the special forces soldiers stop to help him, if he fell? Or would they leave him in the forest and pretend they hadn't missed him in their haste, until it was too late to double back?

Stay with them!

Tripada had not come this far and taken these extraordinary risks to miss the final showdown with his enemy. He had tracked Garuda Malajit for two long, dreary years, always a step or two behind the Sword of Freedom's psychopathic leader as they danced around a giant chess board, using men of flesh and blood as pawns. It was infuriating and reflected badly on his own skills as a government enforcer.

In the quiet hours of the night, when he was honest with himself, Tripada knew that he would be replaced soon if he didn't get results. This night he would be vindicated, all his past embarrassments obliterated by the fresh blood of his enemies.

But first, he had to reach the battle site alive.

It troubled him that he was winded, when they'd covered less than half the distance to their destination. Those around him seemed to feel no strain, although they grunted softly now and then, when one of them collided with a tree or tripped over a dangling vine. How young they were, and capable of anything.

Including sweet revenge, Tripada guessed, if he pushed them too far.

He'd have to watch his own men, therefore, when they met the enemy. It would be easy for a "stray" bullet to find him in the dark, and who would be the wiser? Who would call for a ballistics test on friendly weapons, or believe his death was anything beyond a tragic accident if it were proved that one of his own men had fired the shot?

Tripada knew there'd be no test and no inquiry if he died this night. As long as Malajit and his guerrillas were destroyed, the generals in Jakarta would be satisfied. Indeed, they might even prefer if he was killed in battle. All the better to avoid promoting him, placing Tripada in position to avenge the slights he'd suffered at their hands.

He stumbled on a root and skinned his palm against a nearby trunk, but kept himself from falling. The commandos on his heels did not break stride. Tripada labored to keep pace, drawing his inspiration from the fact that he could hear the sounds of automatic weapons much more clearly now. They were within a quarter mile of contact with the enemy, he guessed, and closing rapidly.

Watch everyone. Trust no one.

Precautions.

They would all be wasted when they reached the battleground. That much he knew from past experience. No matter how a military thrust was charted and rehearsed, Tripada understood that something always went awry.

But he could fix it. He could save himself and his career. A simple gift for his superiors would make the difference.

Malajit's head, perhaps.

Inside a picnic basket.

Buoyed by the image in his mind, Tripada found his second wind and charged on toward the fateful meeting with his enemy.

JASON CLARIDGE HAD memorized the spot where the guerrillas had his parents chained. It was emblazoned in his mind, as clearly written there as if he'd fed coordinates into a GPS receiver and got his marching orders from the great eye in the sky.

Marking the spot and reaching it, however, were two very different things. For one thing, there were forty-odd strangers bent on killing him before he reached his goal. He'd dropped a few of them already, but they still weren't running short of men or guns.

Another problem was his need to track Matt Cooper through the bloody chaos of the killing ground. It would take both of them to extricate his parents, one for each, and Claridge couldn't see him at the moment, as he fought his way across the camp.

The third problem—assuming they succeeded with the first two steps and found his parents still alive—was getting out. The back side of the plan was weak, in Claridge's opinion. It rested on a host of shaky suppositions, and if any one of them proved wrong, the plan was doomed. But it seemed to be the only possibility.

They had to reach his parents, release them from their chains, and move them across the southern half of the guerrilla camp, fight their way past any sentries posted there and reach the jungle safely, where they would have to elude pursuit until Cooper arranged a pickup.

Nothing to it, right?

A bullet sang past Jason's face, not grazing close, but near enough for him to feel its slipstream on his painted cheek. He didn't bother looking for the shooter, knew it was a waste of time best spent on churning toward his goal and dropping anyone who blocked his path.

As he charged, the carbine's slide locked open on an empty

chamber. The guy in front of him was only wounded, staggering from the impact of a bullet in his shoulder while he tried to level his Kalashnikov. Claridge kept going, didn't even try reloading on the run with barely ten yards separating them. He was a juggernaut, drawing the rifle back to swing it like a baseball bat, praying for a grand slam.

The CAR-15's stock met his adversary's face with crushing force, wrenching the rebel's whole head sharply to his right. Claridge had no idea if his opponent was disabled or deceased, but he went down all right, firing a short burst toward the tree line as he fell.

Reload now!

Thought and action were as one, his knees still pumping as he ran flat-out across the clearing that had turned into a slaughterhouse. He ditched one mag, plucked another from the bandolier across his chest and rammed it home without once glancing at his weapon.

Ready.

Just in time.

Two more rebels were crouching in his path, distracted by some action on their flank, but wising up to Claridge's presence as he closed the gap. One had an AK, but the other was palming a machete in his rush to join the fight.

Bring a knife to a gunfight, and what do you get?

He stitched them both with 5.56 mm rounds, enough to do the job without extravagance. He'd need whatever ammunition he could muster as the night wore on, and wasting it would be a critical mistake.

He glimpsed the shelter that hid his parents, the way still blocked by men and prostrate bodies, screened by battle smoke. But he could see them.

In another moment, maybe two, they would see him.

He fired from the hip at his human roadblocks, unaware of the challenge that came from his lips.

"Coming through!" Claridge shouted. "Get out of the way! Coming through, you bastards!"

AMOS CLARIDGE SHOUTED, "It is His judgment!" as another blast of thunder rocked the infidels around him. Surging to his feet, he spread his arms, threw back his head and shouted to the night, "Praise Jesus!"

Merilee was tugging at his sleeve, trying to draw him back inside their lean-to. "Amos, stop this! You'll be killed!"

"He told us, woman." Amos turned a beatific smile upon his wife, blind to her weeping. "No more rain. The fire, this time!"

"Amos—"

Dismissing her, he turned back to the figures running every which way, bumping into one another, brandishing their guns as if a piece of iron could stay the wrath of God.

"Give up, you sinners, and repent!" he shouted after them. "The day of judgment is at hand!"

Some of them gaped at him in passing, as if he was an attraction in a sideshow. Amos beamed at all of them alike, his smile a glimmering rebuke.

"Pray for your enemies and for those who despitefully use you!" he cried. "Yes, I've done that, Lord. But they don't listen to your word. They're heathens, Lord! Blasphemers! You've prepared a fiery place for them, dear Father, and they're ready to burn!"

Amos was walking as he spoke, but suddenly he came up short, unable to proceed. He glanced down at his ankle, wrapped in a chain, and frowned as if the sight surprised him. Merilee was at his side now, using all her strength to draw him after her, back toward the small half-tent they shared.

"Amos, for God's sake—"

"Yes! For His sake, I must give these infidels one last

chance to redeem themselves, before they're cast into the lake of fire to suffer torment everlasting."

The night was filled with hornets, buzzing angrily around his head. They were invisible by firelight, but their sound invigorated Amos. He was buoyed by the fact that they ignored him, stinging others here and there throughout the camp. Their sting was powerful enough to knock men down.

"The prophecy's fulfilled!" he said. "The Book of Revelation's come to life! Oh, Lord, thank you for granting me the privilege of witnessing these final days."

One of the infidels ran up to Amos, shouting in a language that the missionary didn't understand. He held some kind of rifle, jabbing it at Amos in a perfect rage.

"Brother," Amos cautioned him, "you would be well advised to place your trust in God, and not the things of mortal man."

Wild-eyed, the gunman raised his weapon, sighting down its barrel. Amos stared into its muzzle, less than eighteen inches from his face. It should have meaning for him, this he knew, but what it meant eluded him.

"God loves a cheerful giver!" he declared.

The gunman made some inarticulate response, and then a miracle occurred before the preacher's very eyes. One of the hornets that were swarming everywhere around the camp collided with the shooter's head and flew completely through it, spraying gray-flecked crimson from the other side.

"Praise Jesus!" Amos shouted. "A thousand shall fall at my right hand, and ten thousand at my left hand, but the shadow of Death shall pass me by. Glory hallelujah!"

Merilee threw herself upon him then, thin arms wrapping around his neck, one leg twisted around his, as if to drop him with a judo throw. They grappled for a moment, Amos plucking at her hands in wry bemusement, while she cried for him to join her in the tent.

"There's no time, woman," he retorted. "We must put all mortal passions from our hearts and minds. God calls us to a higher purpose now. Don't fight Him! Yield and be redeemed!"

They fell together, struggling on the ground, while all around them strangers fought and died. Amos was jarred and startled by the fall. His new perspective on the battleground made the combatants look like giants.

"Save us, Lord, from the behemoth!"

One of them rushed toward him, then leaped over Amos as if he was simply one more body littering the ground. One of the raging hornets caught the runner in midair and pitched him backward, tumbling over Amos and Merilee as he fell. The impact stunned Amos, left him dazed and breathless.

"Jesus, spare us!" Wheezing, as he raised his arms in supplication. "We've been faithful. You above all others must know that!"

Merilee clung to him as if she were lost at sea, and Amos was her life raft, pleading with him. "Amos! Stop, for *my* sake!"

His mind switched gears, no warning to it, and the fear was suddenly upon him. Trembling helplessly, he felt the tears spring to his eyes. "Oh, Lord," he wept, "send us a champion, I beg of you."

A shadow fell across him, and when Amos dared to raise his eyes, he saw a tall man with a painted face, all streaked with green and black.

The figure spoke.

"Pop! Mom! Are you all right?"

BOLAN WAS HALFWAY to the captives when a corpse sat up and tackled him. The guy was strong for a dead man, and his weight threw Bolan off balance, taking him down before he had time to react.

There was an art to falling gracefully, one of the first things taught in any martial arts class, but it didn't always work. This time gravity, momentum and the 165-pound anchor lashed to Bolan's left leg got the better of him. He hit the ground hard, nearly losing his grip on the Steyr AUG, while his gear dug painfully into his ribs.

Bolan rolled and kicked out at the guy with his right foot, missing the guerrilla's head but landing a solid blow to his shoulder. It won a grunt from his attacker, squeezed between clenched teeth, but the human limpet held fast. A second kick peeled back a strip of bloody scalp and made the rebel snarl.

Bolan reversed the AUG, just as his enemy reached up to grasp his web belt, groping for whatever weapons he could reach. The guy looked up at Bolan as the muzzle touched his forehead, then his face erupted with the grisly blowback from the Steyr's muzzle-blast.

The third kick freed him, and the Executioner was on his feet again, reoriented in a heartbeat, moving toward the point where he had last seen the Claridges. He had no idea if they were still alive, much less fit to travel, but finding out was the point of the game.

A shooter lurched into his path, half-blinded by a scalp wound that had drawn a veil of blood across his face. He held a short-barreled revolver, some cheap knockoff of a Smith & Wesson, waving it in front of him with no clear fix on who he planned to shoot. The piece came up as Bolan charged him, both hands clutching it as he thumbed back the hammer and prepared to fire.

Too late.

Three 5.56 mm tumblers ripped into his chest with chainsaw force and canceled any worries the guerrilla may have had about his eyesight. Bolan dodged around the crumpling body, past him even as he fell, fixed firmly on his goal—until a shout rose from the trees behind him, and another wave of automatic fire opened on the rebel camp.

He broke stride, turning, as a line of cammo-clad commandos burst from the forest, howling battle cries and firing from the hip as they advanced. Taken completely by surprise, the nearest rebels were cut down like stalks of corn before a thresher.

Bolan knew regulars on sight. For one thing, all of their equipment matched, and there were no blue jeans or hand-patched khaki trousers mixed in with the camouflage fatigues. They also carried M-16 assault rifles, which marked their link to Uncle Sam.

No time to waste.

The new arrivals didn't seem intent on taking prisoners. Perhaps they saw a chance to end a major threat once and for all, or maybe they just loved their work. In either case, Bolan didn't intend to be a target in their shooting gallery.

The regulars changed things, but Bolan's problem was the same: get the hostages out of there alive, without inflicting any needless trauma in the process.

Dodging bullets, charging through the smoke and dust, he wondered whether he was already too late.

14

Mahmoud Kendik was terrified. He'd missed his chance to break out from the special forces column during their last sprint to battle, and now he was part of the mad dash over open ground, shouting and firing at the enemy.

Except that Kendik wasn't armed.

He shouted all the same, waving his arms like a madman, as if extravagance would stop the bullets finding him and snuffing out his life.

It seemed to work, at first. Tripada's soldiers were completely unexpected, their onslaught as surprising to the Sword of Freedom rebels as a marching band or troupe of elephants might be. Their first barrage of automatic fire cut through the nearest ranks and left torn bodies twitching on the ground before their targets could react.

Despite the rush, the thunder all around him, part of Kendik's mind was still distracted by a question. Why were all the rebels firing guns before the regulars arrived? Who were their targets? What in hell was happening?

Kendik could see only Malajit's guerrillas in the camp, yet all of those still on their feet had weapons and were firing rounds in one direction or another, seemingly without coherent thought. A moment later, roughly half of them zeroed their smoking weapons on Tripada's skirmish line and blazed away with everything they had.

Kendik's hoarse shouting became a squeal of panic as the bullets whined around him, high and low. The soldier on his left was hit and staggered, slumping to the ground. Impulsively, Kendik reached down and snatched the M-16 from twitching fingers.

Kendik wasn't good with guns. He'd never been a violent man, per se, always preferring guile and trickery when options were presented. He had fired a pistol once, at targets on a client's private shooting range, but this was his first time holding an automatic weapon.

Never mind. At least he could defend himself.

The charge had carried them into the camp and past the scattered line of bodies mown down by the column's first barrage. Tripada's soldiers broke formation then, perhaps sensing that it was suicide to trust parade ground rules when frantic enemies surrounded them on every side. By breaking off in twos and threes, they could protect themselves and stalk their adversaries through the smoky chaos of the camp.

As for Mahmoud Kendik, he simply wanted to survive.

And that would be no simple task.

First thing, he dropped and ducked into a tent, knowing that it wouldn't stop a bullet, but it would conceal him for the moment and allow the nearest shooters to seek other targets while he hid. A moment later, he recoiled and spilled into the open, reeling from the dead man with the mangled face who occupied the tent.

Allah, save me!

There was no reply, of course. Kendik and Allah hadn't been on speaking terms since Kendik had been old enough to recognize that the Almighty had deserted him to grow or starve in the heart of a pitiless slum.

It was a reflex, nothing more, that made him call on Allah now. Mahmoud Kendik knew he could count on no one but himself, if he intended to survive the night.

Step one, he thought, was getting out of there, as far away as possible before some lunatic on one side or the other noticed him and dropped him in his tracks. Tripada's men were busy, heedless of his movements, but the rebels posed a danger, since he wore a version of the standard army uniform. Even the ones who might've recognized him in civilian clothes, from his prior visits to their company, would try to kill him now without a second's hesitation.

He wanted to escape, but retreating from the camp still meant exposure. He would have to stand, then run, showing his back to the guerrillas and Tripada's men alike. Any rebel who noticed his flight would see a government coward, a target ripe for the picking. Tripada's regulars, meanwhile, might think he was deserting and unleash a hail of fire as punishment.

Crawl.

It might've been humiliating, under different circumstances, but he saw no shame in creeping underneath the crisscross streams of automatic fire. Kendik had seen professionals do much the same in training. Never mind that he was crawling away from the battle, while soldiers were taught to creep toward it.

One man's cowardice was another's common sense.

It was damned slow going, even though he hadn't traveled far inside the hostile camp. Kendik had to detour around corpses and men close to death, some of the latter reaching out to clutch at him, as if they thought he was a corpsman come to heal them. When they stuck, he pried their fingers loose, cursing despite the tremor in his voice.

Bullets came close from time to time. One burst tore up the sod immediately to his left and spat mud in his face, stinging one eye and leaving Kendik with a foul taste in his mouth.

Forget it.

If he reached the nearest town alive, there would be wine enough to wash the taste of mud and death out of his mouth.

But first he had to reach the trees, the darkness that would shelter him. Creeping across the soil chewed up by boots and bullets, Kendik didn't know if he could make it. Every yard he gained was progress, but it also made him feel as if a great ax poised above him was about to fall.

At last, he reached the point where firelight gave way to the night. Bolting erect, he sprinted for the trees, breath rasping in his throat.

Kendik never heard the shot that drilled between his heaving shoulder blades and slammed him facedown to the earth.

"JASON? WHAT ARE YOU doing here?"

"No time for that now, Mom. I need to get you out of here."

"But how—?"

"No time!"

"My boy?" His father's voice was cracked and tremulous. "Is that my boy?"

The chain was solid. Jason Claridge tugged it twice, with all his strength, then gave up when he heard his father make a little groaning noise. The padlock was sturdy.

"Okay, stand back," he told his parents. Nodding toward the shelter half, he added, "Get back under there."

His father didn't seem to understand, but Jason's mother pulled him after her. They crouched together under canvas, while he knelt in front of them and aimed his carbine at the padlock.

Risky.

Any rounds he fired at tempered steel could ricochet, maybe come back to bite his own ass if he wasn't careful. Still, there seemed to be no options, since he hadn't brought a hacksaw or a cutting torch along on his hike through the Borneo jungle.

And they were definitely running out of time.

Where was Cooper?

Never mind. You're here. Do it!

He fired one round, then followed up with two more when the first one didn't do the trick. On three, the lock cracked open and he ripped it free, scorching his fingertips on heated metal in the process.

That released his parents from the stake that held them tethered, but the chain was still padlocked to his father's left ankle, his mother's right. Jason couldn't blast those, so close to their legs that any piece of shrapnel could crack bone or slice veins. But maybe...

"Here's the plan," he told them, speaking chiefly to his mother. "I can't blow the locks on your ankles, but maybe I can cut the chain a few links out on either side. That would let you run, at least."

If they *could* run. He'd never seen his parents look so thin and haggard, as if they'd aged fifty years since he last saw them.

"Cut the chain," his mother said. "We'll run, all right."

"Okay, watch your eyes. Mom first."

The SEAL stepped on the chain, pulling it taut on one side of his mother's leg, even as he placed his own leg between her and his carbine. It wasn't much help, but every little bit counted.

The first round didn't snap the chain, so he set the CAR-15 for 3-round bursts and gave it two, raising a little cloud of dust around their feet. When he could see the chain again, one of its links was cut and twisted open, showing shiny steel beneath a layer of rust.

One down, and four to go.

He had to cut the chain on each side of the shackled legs, so that they wouldn't wind up dragging fifteen feet of chain behind them, through the forest. It was easier the second time, now that he had the hang of it, and in another moment, his mother was free of her literal bond to the rebel encampment.

"Now Pop," Jason said, stepping close to his father.

"My boy?" The aging man who stood before him seemed confused, as if his mind had lost its grip on simple things.

"It's me. Cover your eyes, Pop."

Jason aimed, fired—and the CAR-15 burned up its last two rounds without cutting the chain. He dropped the empty magazine, had a replacement in his left hand when he heard his mother cry, "Watch out!"

Jason glanced up and saw one of the rebels rushing at him with his AK-47 raised, as if to swing it like a club. He dropped the magazine and raised his carbine, braced in both hands to absorb the blow.

I guess we all ran out of bullets.

It reminded him of cudgel matches, back in basic training, but the other guy had never tried to kill him in those practice exercises. This one meant to split his skull and Jason was trying to return the favor with a minimum of wasted time.

He blocked another caveman swing and lashed out at his adversary with a groin kick, missing by a fraction of an inch. It still rocked his opponent, though, and Jason took advantage of the moment to mash the shooter's nose with a buttstroke from his carbine. When the rebel fell, Jason crouched over him and slammed his weapon twice into the loser's larynx.

Finished.

He avoided looking at his mother as he retrieved the rifle magazine, wiped it and hastily reloaded his carbine.

"Okay, Pop. Here we go."

"My boy."

Two point-blank bursts, and it was done.

"That's it," he said. "We're getting out of here."

A shadow loomed beside him, Jason turning with his finger on the trigger, ready for the kill.

"My sentiments exactly."

"I WAS ABOUT TO WRITE you off," the SEAL replied.

"I got hung up," Bolan said.

"And you're hit." Jason pointed.

Two fingers came back bloody from his scalp. "It's nothing. We should go right now."

"I heard that."

Turning to his parents, Jason said, "Mom, Pop, it's time to split."

"You young people these days," the old man said.

Smiling.

That one's gone, Bolan thought, asking, "Can he run?"

"We'll soon find out. Still the river?"

"Unless you know a better way."

"Not me." Grim-faced, the young man told his parents, "Follow him. I'm right behind you."

"If the Lord had meant for man to—"

"Not now, Amos!" snapped the woman. "Move!"

It was a relatively short run to the river, but the war was all around them, now that regulars and rebels had engaged, some of them grappling hand-to-hand. It was a gamble, but if they could make it out of camp and reach the water, find some darkness that would cover them, they had a fighting chance.

Fighting was the operative word, as Bolan led their foursome through the battleground to Hell's back door. Each time combatants strayed too close, he hit them with a short burst from the AUG and put them down. He drew no line based on their uniforms, any more than the regular strike team had tried to protect the two prisoners.

Behind him, he heard Jason's carbine hammering at targets on their flanks and to the rear. It might've been a hopeless fight, surrounded as they were, without the new arrivals keeping the guerrillas busy.

Providence? Or pure, dumb luck?

Halfway to cover, Bolan heard a woman's cry behind him. Spinning, he found Amos Claridge on the ground, clutching a leg, his wife kneeling beside him. Blood was seeping from between the preacher's fingers.

"Let me see the wound," Bolan said, leaning in. A burst of 5.56 mm fire told him Jason had canceled out another close-range threat.

Merilee Claridge pulled her husband's hands away, cooing her reassurance as he moaned. The shot was in-and-out, blood welling from both sides, but there was no spray from a severed artery.

"He can't walk, now," the preacher's wife said, softly weeping.

"It's okay. I've got him," Jason told his mother, stooping to hoist his father in a fireman's carry. The old man seemed to weigh nothing. The grimace on Jason's face, when he met Bolan's gaze, had nothing to do with the physical strain.

"Are we good?" Bolan asked him.

The SEAL gripped his father with one hand, his weapon in the other. "We're good to go," he said.

And so they went, with Bolan leading, Merilee behind him, Jason on the rearguard with his father draped across one shoulder. They could hear Amos babbling as they ran, no pain apparent in his voice as he reeled off disjointed Bible verses.

His mind's gone. Bolan wondered if it might not be a blessing in disguise. The preacher couldn't cut it in this world, bereft of godly thoughts and deeds, so he shut down and slipped into another realm where quoting scripture made the bad things go away. It posed no problem at the moment, but they'd have to muzzle him once they were in the jungle, so his nonsense sermon didn't beckon hunters to pursue them.

One step at a time.

They hadn't reached the river yet, much less the so-so safety of the forest. They still had eighty yards or so to cover, but most of the shooters who would otherwise have tried to stop them were distracted by the task of fighting for their lives.

Most, but not all.

Ahead of them, three rebels had been quick and slick enough to dig themselves a shallow foxhole for protection, sniping from cover at any targets they could find. The excavation lay in Bolan's path, and even as he noticed it, the shooters noticed him.

No time for detours.

Bolan fired a burst to keep their heads down, followed by a frag grenade to put them out of action. Instead of warning Merilee, he pulled her down beside him in a crouch, while Jason saw the danger for himself and knelt beside them. Four long seconds later, the grenade exploded and the shouting from the foxhole turned to garbled screams.

"Clear!" Bolan said, and rushed the hole ahead of his companions. He could see one shooter moving, but there was no system to it, jerky thrashing, and he didn't waste a bullet as they passed.

A moment later, they were on the riverbank and running toward the darker shadows of the forest.

"This way!" Bolan said, leading the pack westward.

"Thank God, we're free!" gasped Jason's mother, as the jungle closed around them, muffling the sounds of combat still ongoing in the rebel camp.

"Not yet," Bolan said, correcting her.

And in his mind, a solemn voice repeated it.

Not yet.

GARUDA MALAJIT WAS in a perfect frenzy, raging at his men, the enemy, the very world around him. Everything that he had fought for, risked his life for, seemed about to crumble and slip through his hands like dust. The regulars had found his camp, might well annihilate his men, and the prisoners were gone.

It was too much.

Malajit had lost his little team of shooters when the special forces strike force rushed the camp. He'd sent them off to face the enemy, while he went on to fetch the hostages. At that point, he'd still harbored some idea that the Americans could get him out of this, but they were gone.

Where did they go?

No matter. He could see the chains were broken and his last chance had disappeared. He hoped they'd meet a gruesome death, wherever they had gone. It was no more than they deserved, for ruining his plans.

He raged against the damned unfairness of it all, seeing his dream in smoking ruins, knowing it could never be recaptured. Malajit had lost the chance to save his people and his nation. More importantly, he had forever lost the chance to be a hero, to make history and live in royal opulence.

All gone.

In his demented fury, Malajit lashed out at everyone around him. He had no more allies. There were only enemies who sought to kill him, and the traitors who had failed to keep his dream alive. Malajit hated all of them with equal bitterness, and he would gladly kill them all if he had time and opportunity.

Where was Shaitan Takeri when he needed help? Most likely rotting in the jungle, with a bullet in his head. Good riddance. Let the others join him, then, for failing Malajit and sacrificing his great vision for himself.

One of his soldiers ran toward Malajit, calling his name. He had no weapon, but he recognized a friend. The shock on that young face was palpable as Malajit raised his Kalashnikov and fired a burst into the runner's chest.

One traitor down. How many left to go?

As Malajit moved through the killing ground, he babbled curses, maledictions, any insult he could think of to describe the scum around him. He shot a wounded special forces soldier next, and then another of his own men who pretended innocence and pleaded for his life.

Bastards.

They'd teamed up to betray him, then they'd fallen out and set to killing one another. Malajit would help them, but it wouldn't bring his plans back from the dead.

If he could find the preacher, though...

He ran back to the place where he'd last seen the preacher, crouching in the battle smoke to see the broken chains. Bright cartridge cases on the ground told Malajit someone had freed the prisoners and taken them away.

But where?

If they had left the camp, his last hope vanished with them. Still, they might be hiding near at hand. If Malajit could sniff them out, there was a chance to save himself.

He rose, turned from the lean-to and the chains, scanning the battlefield. There were more bodies than the last time he had checked, more wounded writhing on the ground. Fewer men of either side still on their feet and fighting now.

A movement on his left brought Malajit around, clutching his AK-47. Twenty feet away, a man in government fatigues stood facing him.

"It's you at last," the stranger said.

Malajit reckoned he should know that face. There was something about it. He had studied it for some reason, in photographs.

"Ah. Major Tripada."

"I suppose I should be flattered."

"Hardly. You're wounded."

"Nothing serious," Tripada said, flapping his bloody left arm like a broken wing. "It means another medal, plus the one I'll get for killing you."

"I'm glad you've come," said Malajit. "I sent men out to kill you twice before, but you were lucky."

"I still am," the major assured him.

"Not tonight."

"I've always thought you were insane," Tripada said. "Just look around you. Where's your army? You have nothing left."

Except the hope of resurrection.

Smiling, Malajit replied, "You may yet be surprised."

"Enough of this. You have a choice to make. Surrender and face trial, or die."

"A third choice is to kill you where you stand."

"A man could do it, possibly, but not a worm like you."

The anger surged inside him, boiling through his arms and hands, then through his weapon. Malajit held down the AK-47's trigger, firing the remainder of his magazine. Tripada's M-16 was blazing back at him, and he could feel the bullets stinging him, like gnats.

Like nothing.

When their guns were empty and Tripada had collapsed facedown, Malajit felt a sudden surge of hope. Victorious! He had defeated his opponents once again.

"You can't kill me!" he shouted at Tripada. "It's impossible!"

Smiling, Garuda Malajit slumped forward, dead before he hit the ground.

MERILEE CLARIDGE couldn't quite believe the past half hour. She had been mentally bracing herself to watch Amos die, perhaps in some horrible way, when suddenly she was cast into the midst of an all-out battle. Death seemed certain, if only from stray gunfire, when she and Amos were suddenly rescued—and by their son!

The rest was a blur of sorts. She remembered seeing Jason kill a man, or was it more than one? They'd have to pray about it later, but there wasn't time right now. She knew there had been running—she was still running, in fact—and Amos had been wounded in the leg. Outside the camp at last, there had been hasty first-aid measures taken to prevent more bleeding from that wound, and then more running for their lives.

After the long days and nights of captivity, she could hardly believe they were free. Not safe, of course. She wouldn't stretch a point that far, but clearly better off than they had been an hour earlier.

If something happened to them now, she could truly say it was God's will. He had let her see Jason again, and what more could she ask?

Not safe, a small voice in her mind repeated, nagging her. Not yet.

She slowed her pace, not tired so much as curious. The others pulled away from her a bit, as she turned back to stare along the rough trail they had followed from the camp. There was the river, and the jungle close around them.

What had changed?

She heard someone calling to her, softly. "Mrs. Claridge! It's too soon to stop!"

The words slipped out unplanned, almost as if they'd come from someone else. "There's someone coming after us," she told him.

The big man was beside her now, and she could hear that Jason had stopped on the trail, bearing his father's weight in stoic silence.

"Where?" he asked. "Did you see them?"

"Not exactly." Try as she might, Merilee couldn't take her eyes from the darkness behind them. It seemed to be closer now, if such a thing were possible. "It's more like I feel them."

The stranger didn't laugh at her or take her arm to drag her. He waited, poised and listening, until a kind of crackling noise from the jungle made his shoulders slump.

"You're right," he said.

Turning to Jason in the dark, he whispered, "We've got a tail."

"How many?" Jason asked, moving to join them.

"I'm not sure. Best guess, no more than five or six."

"You want to take them here?"

"It's still too close. We've got a lead. Let's stretch it for another mile or so and see what we can find to make a better setup."

"Right." The hand upon her arm was Jason's. "Let's go, Mom. We're wasting time."

More running, then, and Merilee was suddenly fatigued. She wondered if that brief stop on the trail had been enough to undermine her stamina. She hadn't been this tired before, surely. Or maybe she'd been running on adrenaline and fear.

It seemed a cruel trick, letting them escape from their tormentors, only to send others after them, to run them down. If there'd been time to sit and think about it, Merilee might have been angry, but the hectic demands of the moment prevented her from venting, or even focusing much on herself.

She thought of Amos, maybe dying, very possibly insane, and wondered if he even knew his boy had rescued them from their oppressors. As for Jason, she wondered why he was there too.

Am I about to lose them both? My husband and my son?

And this other man, who was he, exactly? He was older than Jason, clearly more experienced in combat, but Jason called him "Cooper" not "sir" the way he'd been trained to address all superior officers. Then again, perhaps Cooper wasn't even in the Navy. Maybe he was…something else.

A guardian angel?

Why not? She reckoned it would be a miracle if all of them came through the night alive.

A miracle.

Did she have faith enough to hope, much less believe?

She lurched to a halt when Cooper and Jason stopped running. Amos was quiet now, unmoving. She hoped he was unconscious, for all their sakes. The last thing they needed now was a crazy sermon shouted at the top of his lungs.

"Suits me fine," Jason agreed.

Merilee looked around them, trying to see how this patch of jungle differed from the last, but its details escaped her.

"Mom?" Jason was calling her. "I'll put Pop over here. Stay with him and stay down, all right? No matter what."

"All right, dear."

Now, up close, she saw that several trees had fallen on each side of the trail. Jason had lowered Amos to the shelter of a log some distance from the trail. She joined him, touched her son's cheek as he turned away, and settled in beside her husband. Closer to the trail, Jason and Cooper were selecting places for themselves, checking their weapons, making ready for another fight.

If only there was something she could do to help them.

"Our Father," she whispered, "who art in Heaven…"

IT ALL CAME DOWN to this.

The Executioner was crouched behind a log that ferns and weeds had overgrown, until its character was lost and it acquired the aspect of an upthrust ridge. The soft sounds of the river on his right combined with still more drizzling rain would mask the sounds of their pursers, but Bolan had no doubt that they were coming.

Closer to his parents, on the far side of the trail, Jason had found a similar crude barricade, and Bolan trusted that he would be ready when the trouble broke. He'd proved himself to Bolan's satisfaction, and the Executioner could only hope all of them would make it through the night alive. If not, at least the death that waited for them here was quick and relatively clean.

He didn't know which side had sent the hunting party after them, and Bolan didn't care. He had performed the first part of his mission, extrication of the captives, but the job would not be done until they were delivered safely to some friendly settlement. Whether that part could be achieved or not, he wasn't sure.

He wished for Jack Grimaldi, then, but wishes wouldn't cut it. There was no time to deploy the satellite communications gear, and no confirmed coordinates to offer. In any case, Grimaldi couldn't bail them out of their predicament. He wasn't flying cover on this mission, only pickup. And the battle would be over by the time he got his chopper in the air.

The trackers had become impatient. Bolan heard them now, much closer than the last time. Impatience was good. It commonly produced mistakes, and those were sometimes fatal.

He waited, cheek pressed against the AUG's plastic stock, scanning the night in front of him. He had agreed with Jason that they ought to let their enemies approach as close as possible, scope out the numbers if they could, and try to make it quick. The risk in that was having hostile guns so close they barely had to aim, but if he did it properly—

The first hunter emerged from darkness on the left side of the trail. Another walked behind him, and another behind that. As they approached, Bolan checked out the right side— his side—and discovered three more moving toward his post in single file.

Six adversaries in the darkness. They'd already faced and beaten greater odds, not once, but several times. It hardly seemed a challenge, but he knew the risks that came attached to overconfidence.

Bolan was good, but he was not infallible. Like anybody else, he made mistakes, but he did not repeat them. And he always learned a lesson from his failures. So far, he had managed to survive.

So far.

Was one of these six enemies the man who'd take him out? Somewhere on Earth, he knew, there was a faster gun, a stronger hand, a sharper eye. Every time he took another mission he was inching closer to that day.

Nobody beat the odds forever.

Nobody got out of life alive.

There hadn't been much time, but he and Jason had devised a basic plan. Aside from waiting for their enemies to move in close, they planned to slam the door behind them, spook their adversaries into rushing forward when they least expected it. Off balance and disoriented, they should then be easy prey.

Dead meat.

At thirty yards, Bolan unhooked his final frag grenade and pulled the pin. Across the trail, if they were synchronized, Jason was doing likewise. Bolan let the enemy patrol move closer, shaving ten yards off the gap, before he made the pitch.

Bombs away.

Bolan settled back onto the Steyr and framed one of the stalkers in his optical sight. The numbers were running in his head, counting backward from six.

He couldn't tell if the hunters heard either grenade hit the ground. They didn't flinch or react, may have missed them entirely, but they couldn't miss the double blast of fire and shrapnel that went off behind them. They lurched forward, then crouched, some of them turning back in the direction of the blasts, defensive now.

Bolan dropped the nearest of them with a 3-round burst to the chest. The guy went down like a cutout silhouette in a carnival shooting gallery, dropping backward silently, as if the turf had been yanked out from under his feet.

The next one in line started laying down fire. It was all panic reflex, but his rounds still came too close for comfort, smacking into Bolan's log and clipping ferns on either side of him.

Too close.

The Steyr had a built-in flash suppressor, but it wasn't perfect. Maybe the hunter had seen the rifle's muzzle-flash, or maybe not. He saw the second one, for damned sure, as a swarm of 5.56 mm manglers found him in the dark and punched him through a jerky little dance.

The dead-end two-step.

Jason was firing away to Bolan's left, taking fire in return. Bolan couldn't help him yet, with one of his own targets still in the game.

His third mark was retreating, firing short bursts to cover his withdrawal, but Bolan couldn't let him get away. No matter who had sent the hunting party out, he wanted them to wait a while, before they understood that the arrangement had gone sour. No stragglers running back to camp for reinforcements this time.

Not if he could help it.

His mark was ducking toward the river, seeking cover there, when Bolan fired again. It wasn't clean, but he still scored a hit, drilling his target through the right side of his upper chest. Not fatal, probably, but there was shock enough behind it that the gunner stumbled, lost his weapon and wound up on his knees.

Going nowhere fast.

Bolan's next burst finished him. He held the mark and watched the dead man topple over on one side, across the trail. Whoever followed after the patrol would find him there, unless the scavengers moved in and dragged him someplace private for a snack.

More firing on his left, and Bolan turned in time to see Jason take down their final adversary. It had turned into a face-off kind of duel from forty feet or so, but Jason had the cover and it served him well.

Six up, six down.

They waited for another moment, just in case, but there were no more hunters in the woods so far. It was time to move, before another party came along.

"Is that all?" Merilee asked them, when they reached her. "Is it over?"

"I hope so," Bolan told her. "But we've still got quite a hike before we catch a ride."

Epilogue

Jack Grimaldi had been waiting for the squeal, and when it came he asked no questions. He simply noted the coordinates, then frowned on hearing that the pickup would involve four bodies, rather than the three he'd been expecting.

By the time he hit the tarmac, running, he had lost the frown. Four wasn't any stretch for the machine he'd commandeered from Subic Bay, with help from Stony Man Farm. And adding one beat falling short, no doubt about it.

He'd expected three, but feared it might be only two, or Bolan by himself. Hell, why not just admit it? He'd been worried that there'd be no call from Borneo at all. He'd had three hours of sleep per night, the way his nerves had worked on him, but he would make up for it on the down side.

Once he had his people safely home.

The CH-53E Super Stallion was on loan from the Marines at Subic Bay. No trace of their insignia was visible, inside or out, and the call numbers painted on the tail were strictly bogus. Grimaldi was not concerned about legality, but plausible deniability would be preserved at any cost. If he went down, on Borneo or in the drink, the whirlybird he took down with him wouldn't be identified.

Same old, same old.

Mission accomplished. Almost.

Grimaldi worried that they still might have some trouble

on the ground, while they were waiting for him to arrive, but there was nothing he could do to make it any easier. The pickup could be dicey, too, since the Super Stallion had been stripped of all its lethal weaponry at the same time it received the new paint job.

If it came to a showdown, Grimaldi wouldn't be shooting blanks.

He wouldn't be shooting at all.

Winging across the blue, he beamed a silent message to the party waiting for him, still two hours and some-odd minutes out.

Hang on. Help's on the way.

Grimaldi only hoped it wouldn't be too late.

WAITING COULD BE THE worst of it. Before a mission, there was the anticipation of danger and anxiety surrounding unknown factors that could never be accommodated by the best of plans. After, the sweet relief of coming through it all alive could turn to dust, spoiled by the threat of being picked off by some accident or twist of fate, after the worst was past.

But waiting was a game Bolan knew how to play. He spent that time outside himself, evaluating everything around him, from the weather to the plants and animals, terrain, bystanders—anything, in short, that could affect his personal performance when push came to shove.

They had marched through the night to reach their pickup coordinates, with no sign of pursuers on their trail. Bolan knew that didn't mean they were safe. A random patrol could arrive without warning, or the hunters might be quartering the jungle behind them, on foot or in aircraft with heat-seeking gear that would pinpoint their camp from a thousand feet up.

Maybe, but Bolan didn't think so. He believed they'd pulled it off, but there'd be no time for backslapping and congratulations until they were in the air and headed north across the water.

Until then, he'd watch and wait.

His companions, meanwhile, had a family reunion of sorts going on. Bolan tried not to eavesdrop, but some of it still reached his ears. Jason's mother was thankful he'd come, but worried her boy would face punitive action when he returned to his post. Jason urged her not to worry, but Bolan knew how it was with elite fighting units like the SEALs and Green Berets. They might play fast and loose with certain regulations in the field, particularly in a war zone, but on peacetime duty stations discipline was sacrosanct.

That's how they got to be elite, and there was every chance that Jason would be sent down from the unit for his little escapade. That probability could hardly have escaped him, but for now at least, the young man didn't seem to care.

Amos Claridge was hanging on. They'd stopped most of the bleeding from his leg wound, but he couldn't walk unaided. Worse, there'd been no return to lucidity when they were clear of danger, as the Executioner had hoped. When Amos spoke, he quoted scripture in a reedy voice or issued proclamations as if speaking to a congregation. "Repent and be ye saved!" had been his favorite, the past two hours or so, and Bolan wished that he would play another broken record for a while.

The Executioner could only guess what the Claridges had to have suffered in the rebel camp. They both had many injuries, indicating bouts of physical abuse. According to his wife, Amos was marked for execution when they pulled him out, but was the death sentence sufficient to unhinge his mind? Was it the overall experience, or had he been a few bricks shy when it began?

Bolan would leave those questions to the shrinks waiting at Subic Bay, or in the States. It wasn't his place to play armchair analyst for total strangers, and he didn't care to try.

They were still alive. They were going home.

His job would be complete, as soon as Grimaldi picked them up and winged them out of there.

He heard the chopper coming from the north-northeast. Bolan waited, afraid to jump the gun and use his two-way radio too soon, in case it was a hostile bird. The others heard it in another moment, Jason on his feet and reaching for the CAR-15.

Bolan picked up his compact radio and spoke into the mouthpiece. "Eagle, this is Groundhog. Do you read me?"

"Five-by-five," Grimaldi answered. Bolan heard the grin behind his words. "Are those coordinates still good?"

"Affirmative. We're ready when you are, Eagle."

"I'm on my way. Sit tight."

Bolan switched off the radio, beginning to relax a little as he told the others, "That's our ride."

BOLAN RELAXED in the copilot's seat as the helicopter beat its way north skimming blue water en route to the Philippines. The destination wasn't home, but it would do.

Their pickup had been uneventful. Grimaldi couldn't land the chopper at their designated coordinates, but he'd lowered static lines and the elder Claridges had made the first ascent, while Bolan and their son stood guard below. The old man had regained enough strength on the ride upstairs to spout some verses about the ascent into Heaven, but there were no hostile ears in the vicinity to track his voice and bring hellfire down on their heads.

Jason was huddled with his parents in the helicopter's ample cargo bay, with seating for fifty-five soldiers. They'd moved all the way to the back, for a semblance of privacy, and Bolan guessed there'd be tears all around, unless Amos was lost in a glassy-eyed world of his own.

"You think they'll make it?" Grimaldi asked. His voice sounded tinny in Bolan's earphones.

Bolan shrugged. "They've got no wounds that shouldn't heal. On the outside, at least."

"The preacher sounds a little loopy. No offense."

"He lost something back there," Bolan agreed. "Or maybe it's been going for a while. He took some punishment, but whether it's responsible for what you see, who knows?"

"I guess he won't be in the pulpit for a while."

If ever, Bolan thought.

That was the strange thing about faith. The right amount could see a person through the worst of times and bring them out the other side in decent shape. Too much—or faith in the wrong things—could wind up trashing minds and souls.

"Have you heard anything from Hal?" Bolan asked.

"He's been fretting, but you'll never get him to admit it. Toughest mother hen I ever met."

Brognola could breathe easy, now that Bolan and the hostages were on their way to friendly soil. The White House could relax about relations with Jakarta, and some ghost writer in Washington could draft a press release explaining how the Claridges were rescued.

There would be no mention of the Executioner or Stony Man, of course. That would defy the sacred rule of plausible deniability. *We didn't do it* was the creed in Washington, and had been as long as Bolan could remember. *And you can't prove it even if we did.*

"I'm thinking you could use some R and R," Grimaldi said.

"What did you have in mind?"

"Dig this—we get a couple of kayaks and take a week or so to trek the rivers on Luzon. I understand they've got some jungle there you won't believe."

Bolan turned toward Grimaldi with a glare and saw his old friend laughing. "No thanks," he said. "I'll settle for a meal, a bed and twenty hours' sleep."

Grimaldi shook his head. "You had me fooled. I always thought you were adventurous."

"Been there, done that," Bolan replied. "Come get me when you're onto someplace cool and relatively dry."

"I'll work on it."

"Meanwhile, I think I'll get a head start on those twenty hours."

Bolan left his headphones on to mute the chopper's engine noise a bit, and settled back to close his eyes. He might not sleep, but there was peace and healing in the darkness, even so.

He hoped the Claridges would find that peace, that healing, but the matter was out of his hands. Bolan had brought them home, and so his job was done.

For now.

THE
DESTROYER
DARK AGES

LONDON CALLING...

Knights rule—in England anyway, and ages ago they were really good in a crisis. Never mind that today's English knights are inbred earls, rock stars, American mayors and French Grand Prix winners. Under English law, they still totally *rock*. Which is why Sir James Wylings and his Knights Temporary are invading—in the name of Her Majesty.

Naturally, Remo is annoyed. He is from New Jersey. So when Parliament is finally forced to declare the Knight maneuvers illegal, he happily begins smashing kippers...knickers...whatever. Unfortunately, Sir James Wylings responds by unleashing his weapons of mass destruction—and only time will tell if the Destroyer will make history...or be history, by the time he's through.

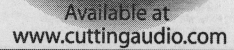